To Joy and all the family for their
encouragement and support.

But at my back I always hear
Times wingèd chariot hurrying near;
And yonder all before us lie
Deserts of vast eternity.

Andrew Marvell
                To His Coy Mistress

DEAR LEONARD

Roger Griffin

Published in 2014 by FeedARead.com Publishing

Copyright © Roger Griffin

A CIP catalogue record for this title is available from the British Library.

TORRINGTON, DEVON, 1960

The boy pulled back the bedclothes and stepped onto the cracked lino, which even in July felt cold to his feet. He picked up the small travel clock from the upturned fruit box that served as his bedside table and bookcase, and switched off the alarm five minutes before it was due to go off and ten minutes before his mother was due to call him. In fact, the alarm clock had never performed its primary function, since the boy always awoke in good time, even on school days when most ten-year-olds yearned for another five minutes in bed. However, this was Sunday, when getting ready for Sunday school could be done at a more leisurely pace, but he was still up early and he would be ready as usual at least thirty minutes before he and his sister left the house for the short walk to the Methodist church.

The boy made his bed neatly, smoothing down any wrinkles in the candlewick bedspread, and placed his current book, Treasure Island (finished by torchlight the night before), between Anna Sewell and Mark Twain. He was relieved to find the bathroom unoccupied by his sister who these days seemed to take longer and longer to get ready and delighted in keeping her brother waiting. After a quick wash, he put on the crisp white shirt, short grey trousers and blue tie that were set out on the landing and went downstairs. His father was peeling potatoes on a sheet of newspaper spread out on the living room table and did not look up when his son entered. The air was thick with domestic tension. The boy always wished that his father would wash the potatoes before peeling them, rather than just putting them straight into the large saucepan at his feet, turning the water browner with each plop.

His mother emerged from the steam of the kitchenette, wiping her hands in her apron. The dinner they would eat on his return from Sunday school was already underway, the dried peas having soaked overnight in their muslin bag, the carrots cut into rounds and the cabbage already bubbling away on the three-ringed cooker. From an early age the boy had wondered why the preparation of vegetables boiled into submission and a piece of over-roasted meat caused so much tension in the house on a Sunday morning. He could already see that his mother was getting one of her migraines as her brow was shiny from rubbing it with Ralgex, her usual standby when faced with the prospect of cooking this hot ritual meal on the warmest day of the year.

'You're going to church on your own today. Your sister's not feeling too chipper.'

'What's the matter with her? She was all right yesterday.'

His mother glanced at her husband who continued his peeling, cutting the larger potatoes to size in the palm of his hand, an action that always made the boy wince.

'She's just not up to it today,' his mother replied. 'Nothing serious.'

'But we always go together...'

'Leave it! You heard your mother.' His father's words stung the boy like the crack of a whip on a horse's withers.

'Tell Mr Welsh that she'll be there next week without fail,' said his mother. 'Now let's be looking at you. Don't pull your trousers up so tight with that belt. You look like a sack tied up in the middle. My goodness, you'll be needing long trousers before too long.'

The boy stepped out into the sunshine and closed the front gate behind him. Every house in the street had its

6

windows open and the air was heavy with the cloying aromas of meat and vegetables mingling with the smells of manure and fresh hay that drifted across the fields behind the village, while snatches of music from tinny radios floated around him. *Cathy's Clown* gave way to *Three Steps To Heaven*. The boy tugged at his collar as the sun caught the back of his neck but he refrained from undoing his top button. On a patch of waste ground a bunch of boys were playing cricket with a homemade bat and a dustbin for a wicket. The hard cork ball hit the bin with a loud metallic thump and the cry of 'howzat' went up in unison as the boy hurried by, his head lowered.

The spire of the small church was already in view as he passed the shops and the Black Horse. He didn't know why he had queried his sister's absence so insistently. He didn't much like his sister these days. What small boy likes an older sister and especially one who was growing away from him faster than the three-year gap between them? Where once he had been the cute little brother, he was now an embarrassment. He used to enjoy sitting with her of an evening as she struggled with her homework (he longed to have homework from his junior school) but lately she had spurned his eagerness to help her. 'Leave me alone! I'd rather get it wrong than have Mr Smarty-pants tell me what to do!'

In the distance the boy could see people emerging from the church after morning service. This was where the children, waiting for Sunday school to begin, kicked their heels outside as the slow exodus of the adults cleared the church before they were allowed to enter. 'Thank you, vicar.' 'Nice sermon, vicar.' He knew all the families that attended church each Sunday. Their forebears had been doing it for generations, sitting uncomfortably in their Sunday best while their elders and betters settled in smug contentment in their family pews at the front. Now the congregation was dwindling fast and evensong was being edged out by the scourge of Sunday bingo.

The boy liked Sunday school partly for the increase in his knowledge, a process that could never be satisfied. He didn't mind that it was mainly Bible knowledge. But he also liked getting his attendance card stamped and looked forward to the certificate of merit, decorated with Holman Hunt's 'Light of the World', that would follow at the end of the year, even though the image of Jesus with the lantern knocking at the moonlit door scared him a bit. His sister liked Sunday school for the seventeen-year-old youth with the Elvis quiff who took some of the lessons and who would lean over her shoulder to point out the salient points in the story of Ruth and Boaz. She was looking forward to getting closer to that quiff when the children had their annual Sunday school outing to Ilfracombe in a couple of weeks.

But today the boy did something that he could never explain. Perhaps it was the unfamiliar absence of his sister at his side or just the heat of a glorious summer's day, shimmering on the tarmac as his footsteps slowed. He was on his own this morning for the first time ever and perhaps he thought he heard a whisper of other possibilities on a day like today, something about making different choices than sitting on a polished bench in a musty church hall. So instead of approaching the church, which was still disgorging its congregation blinking into the sunshine, he turned on his heels and headed out of the village towards the fields. He crossed over the humpbacked bridge under which the local railway line ran, went through a kissing gate and turned down a pathway studded with cowpats, which his polished black shoes carefully avoided, and walked on towards nowhere in particular.

He had dawdled for about ten minutes when he stopped suddenly and looked about him. He could see the heat haze rising above the roofs of the village and the church spire still clearly visible even at this distance. Somehow, at that moment, being where he was in the middle of a field seemed utterly incongruous. He came suddenly to his senses and a shiver of anxiety made his shoulders tremble. At this moment the boy with the quiff and even the vicar would be wondering where his sister and he were. Questions would be asked and soon enough word would reach his mother, if not today, then when she was out shopping in the next few days. If he retraced his steps immediately, or better still, ran back to the church he would admittedly be late but he would be there and he could explain his sister's absence and apologise for his own lateness. But he hesitated because for him being late was worse than not being there at all. He remembered the church Christmas party when his father and mother had had another blazing row before she left the house with the two children in tow. They arrived late at the hall to find the other children halfway through the demolition of all the food and he had to be found a seat away from his friends and given the remnants of curled sandwiches that had already been cleared away. No, it was all too late now and he would just have to get home at the expected time, hoping that no one had said anything and taking the consequences if they had.

The boy stood for a moment wondering how he would spend the time before setting back. He needed to arrive home at the normal time. He didn't notice the group of children who had emerged from the copse to

9

his left and were now stalking him through the waist-high ferns along the path. He heard their rustling and giggling before he saw them launch themselves upon him out of the undergrowth like American marines in a B-movie. The two boys and the gawky girl were familiar to him but they were his sister's age and he had had nothing to do with them since they had left junior school for the local secondary modern. Instinctively, he knew that there was a price to be paid for this chance encounter.

The two lads had no choice but to do something to the younger boy. They were never going to exchange pleasantries with him and just let him go. There were rules of engagement to follow and a pubescent girl to impress. A few shoves, a Chinese burn, a kick in the nuts, perhaps. But first there were pockets to empty. The boy had only a shilling, which was his Sunday school dues, but he gave it up willingly in the hope that he might escape something worse. The two lads disputed over the coin, each trying to grab it from the other, and the boy foolishly took his chance. He turned and ran. If he could get through the kissing gate and beyond, he might get to the main road and the safety of people. But his skinny legs were leaden and he was only halfway to the gate when he was tackled from behind. Unable to put out his hands in time to break his fall, he thudded heavily to the ground, winding himself in the process and grazing his knees on the ash path. Flipped onto his back, he looked up at the body sitting on his chest, its head haloed like some grotesque Virgin Mary. It was the girl who had brought him down so deftly and who now straddled him, panting and grinning. Two bony knees pressed down on his arms painfully, as the lads caught up with the action and fell about to see him felled by a girl.

She was wallowing in her triumph and in no hurry to release her quarry. 'Keep 'is 'ead still,' she cried to the boys as, leaning her body forward, she rubbed her crotch against the boy's mouth and nose and then for good measure she hawked up a gobful of spit and let it drop slowly onto his face.

Dear Leonard,

I'm not sure how I should begin this. I'm not very good at talking about myself - never have been. Soul searching, navel gazing – whatever you want to call it – just isn't my thing. But I need to say something, anything, or I think I might just go crazy - if I'm not already there.

I've known you for a long time but I've never met you, let alone spoken to you. And obviously you don't know me. How could you? I'm speaking to you now because I cannot think of anyone else in the world who could help me. That's pretty sad, isn't it?

How long have I known you? It's over 40 years now. That's a big chunk of someone's life – two-thirds in my case – and in that time you have brought me solace at various times of my humdrum life. A bit of self-pity there, do you think? I'm afraid I'm partial to that; at least that's what Molly thinks. Molly's my wife, by the way. She thinks I have lots of things wrong with me and she's probably right. You know what women are like, always treating a man like a work in progress, always seeking after perfection and never satisfied.

I'm straying from the point. This is not about Molly; it's about me. Harry Dymond, 62 years old, retired for two years, comfortably off, mortgage paid, in good nick apart from a few stiff joints in the morning, with everything to live for and nothing that stirs the least excitement in me. I see the future as a bleak and barren wasteland and if I should pop my clogs before I reach an oasis, no one apart from Molly will give a toss.

I have friends but I tire of them as no doubt they tire of me. Sometimes when I'm in their company I want to scream. It's the sameness: the same jokes, the same stock responses, the same opinions. And I want to scream, not because I despise them, but because I am them.

Molly says that perhaps I should see the doctor. Maybe he will prescribe something that will give me a boost. But I know that pills are not the answer. I have to find the cure within me. Grumpy, tetchy, obsessive old man - heal thyself. But how?

That's when I thought of you, Leonard, someone I admire, revere even, but above all someone I trust. You seem to understand this world better than anyone I know. You have an insight that is unique among men. So, I hope you won't mind if I speak to you from time to time. I don't want to be a bother to you but you are the only person that I can turn to.

Did you say something, Leonard? Sorry, I thought you said something.

CHAPTER 1

'What on earth have you got there?'

Harry did not receive an answer from his wife as she dumped the dirty cardboard box on the kitchen table. But he had a feeling that a second cup of coffee and a morning buried in the Sunday papers were now off the agenda.

'It's such a shame,' she said, pushing the newspapers off the table to accommodate the box. 'Your whole life ending up on a rubbish tip.' She tipped the box over and out spilled a mass of old photos and postcards that she began to spread over the table.

Harry had spent over 40 years exploring his wife's psyche and he knew that this was one of those moments when he was unlikely to get straight answers.

'Molly, why have you been rummaging in Mr Barker's skip?'

Harry knew that strictly speaking it was not Mr Barker's skip because Mr Barker had died nine months before. They had moved next door to the old man five years ago. Having lived in various parts of Cardiff throughout their married life, Molly had decided that the suburb of Heath, with its respectable inter-war houses and parkland, would be their final move, notwithstanding their eventual admission to a residential care home. Mr Barker had been well into his eighties then but was always very sprightly, never seen without a collar and tie, his shoes always polished. Harry and Molly would speak to Mr Barker over the fence of his immaculate garden and Molly in particular would pick up any bulky items of shopping that he needed, although he would never ask directly for help, such was his independence.

But Mr Barker's decline, which seemed to coincide with a fall, had been rapid. He stopped going out and would sit all day at the front window watching the passers-by. He stopped caring for himself and if he did open the door he was unkempt and unshaven. The sluggish machinery of state care creaked into action: meals-on-wheels, home helps and finally a stair lift. When Mr Barker did venture out, which was rare, he had a distracted air about him. Harry remembered finding him walking down the street in his pyjamas, saying over and over again: 'I need to find Joe; I need to find Joe.' Finally, about two years ago Mr Barker had been admitted to a nursing home. The house remained empty during this time and even after his death, when the for-sale sign went up, it seemed to take ages to sell. Someone said that Mr Barker had no living relatives and this had caused the probate process to drag on. Now the house had been finally cleared and they were waiting for their new neighbours to move in.

'Nobody cares any more. Mr Barker would have been so upset to lose all these photographs.'

Harry didn't ask his wife what she intended to do with the contents of the box. They would probably end up in the garage, which still housed so much of his children's stuff even though they had moved out years ago. Whenever they visited, Harry would make a point of referring to his garage as 'the repository' in the hope that they might take some of their stuff with them, but they never did. This would be just another box among so many.

Harry glanced longingly at the newspapers strewn on the floor and wondered if he could sidle off to the conservatory and leave Molly to her task. Just then the phone rang and, seeing that his wife had put on her I'm-very-busy face, he got up to answer it.

'It's Hazel,' he said, 'Billy's come out in a rash and she wants to know what it might be. I'm putting my money on dengue fever.'

Molly gave Harry an old fashioned look and took the phone from him. Harry could now make a quick exit. He knew she would be on the phone to their daughter for at least an hour. He stooped to pick up the newspapers but, as he did, his eye caught a photo that had fallen to the floor. He picked it up and held it momentarily in his fingers. The photo exuded an essence of damp musk, but it was more of a sensation than a smell. It was a sensation from a past world creeping through a chink in time. Harry felt a slight chill run through him as he scrutinised the image.

It was of a young man in military uniform, posed in the formal surroundings of a photographer's studio: stiff-backed chair, potted plant and a foliage-strewn backdrop. On the back of the photograph the words 'To Mother' were written in a steady, confident hand. The face of the subject gave Harry no clues at first until he recognised the upright bearing and air of authority of his former neighbour. Harry delved through the other photos in the box. They were of all sizes and from all eras – the cutting room floor of someone's life: a boy standing proudly with a large horse in a meadow; the same boy, but now older, sitting in front of what looked like an extended family in a large suburban garden, comfortable in their genteel surroundings. Harry started to separate the photos into groups – the boy, the youth, the serviceman – and then a woman began to appear in the photos, here standing self-consciously with a young Mr Barker at a dance, now on their wedding day in the porch of a church. No lavish wedding dress but a serviceable outfit, perhaps the result of pooling precious clothing coupons. He is wearing a demob suit two sizes too big for his now gaunt frame. POW camp perhaps, thought Harry. Here Mrs Barker is holding a sleeping baby and her slightly anxious pose hints at the responsibility that lies ahead; now her husband poses at the seaside with a little boy whose podgy hands grip tightly onto his bucket and spade. In another the fair-haired boy sits proudly in a shiny pedal-car, blinking at the camera.

The Sunday papers now forgotten, Harry began to arrange the photos into a rough chronology; from sepia to black and white, to early colour; from 1920s aunts in cloche hats to Mrs Barker standing outside the house next door in a full 1950s skirt, waving a bunch of keys at the camera, the boy in a striped school blazer standing self-consciously at her side. And then the boy slowly grows up, slicked-back hair turns into a Beatle-cut; a smart Italian suit gives way to tie-dyes and flares, while Mrs Barker moves from a trim twenty-something to a plump matron in crimplene slacks. Mr Barker, however, seems hardly to change at all. He always strikes the same studied pose, with a slight air of detachment from the proceedings. He is never without a collar and tie, even when caught unawares, rubbing oil into his son's cricket bat or trimming the hedge that surrounds the well-kept rear garden. Only the thinning hair marks the passage of time.

The photos also recorded the history of the family's motor cars, which no doubt mirrored Mr Barker's rise up the promotion ladder. Seen gleaming on the drive at various stages are a sturdy Austin A35, a sleek Morris Oxford V and, the final mark of success, a Rover 2000, while Mr Barker, still in collar and tie, ignores the camera as he buffs their wings. Eventually the boy has his own wheels, an open-topped MG Midget with a mini-skirted girl reclining on the bonnet like a showroom model. Harry thought he was up to around the 1970s now, Mr Barker still wearing a suit in most pictures, the bearded boy looking up from under the bonnet of his car, Mrs Barker in garden gloves cutting roses.

Molly returned to the kitchen, having forgotten what she was doing before the phone call from her daughter. The sight of all the photos neatly arranged on the table immediately irritated her.

'I think your grandson has hives, if you're interested.'

Harry knew he was on a loser in the caring grandparent stakes. It was a role most fathers embraced when a daughter had a baby but he had struggled with it from the moment of Billy's birth and he didn't know why.

'Oh, poor chap, I'll ring Hazel later. Don't move the photos, they're in order.'

Molly visibly bristled at the remark.

'In order? What do you mean 'in order'?' Molly spat out the words, her eyes blazing like an animal ready to pounce. 'They're photos, Harry, family photos - not an archive.'

'Is there another box in the skip?' Harry asked. 'These photos just seem to end. There's no more after the 1970s. It doesn't make sense.'

'Look for yourself. I'm going to get the dinner on. Seems like that's all I'm good for.'

Harry went outside to the skip but couldn't really see if it contained any more photos. It was the usual jumble of rubbish, to which passers-by had added their own junk. He wasn't going to delve inside it. While he had hoped for more photos, there was something in his mind that told him he wouldn't find any more.

~

Harry and Molly were sitting in the living room after Sunday lunch drinking coffee. Harry had phoned his daughter, enquired dutifully about Billy's rash and had made peace with his wife by apologising for usurping the box of photos.

'Everything you do has to be so logical, ordered, and in its place,' said Molly between sips. 'You drive me to distraction sometimes. Photos are just people's memories, Harry, and we don't recall memories in a sequence. They're all higgledy-piggledy and jumbled up in our heads. That's all that box of photos is. I only wanted to save them because Mr Barker had no one to keep his memories and he deserved better. But you always have to take a perfectly normal human activity and impose a system upon it, as if doing so will unlock a secret, when all the time it's staring you in the face. You've become very strange of late, Harry, and you're getting worse. I still think you should go to the doctor's. Why don't you just put the box in the garage and be done with it?

Harry nodded to his wife but he wasn't really listening. The box didn't end up in the garage. It went back on the skip. But Harry kept the photos and over the next few days, when Molly was out of the house, he arranged them meticulously in a newly-bought photograph album. He placed the photos in a sequence that reflected his thoughts on their most logical chronology. When he'd finished the task he paused for a moment and, like an antiquarian holding a precious first edition, he traced his fingers along the embossed lettering that spelled out JUMBO PHOTO ALBUM. He then placed the album on the top shelf of his son's old wardrobe, at the back of a pile of football magazines. He told Molly nothing about this because he knew that she just wouldn't understand about such things.

Dear Leonard,

I know my mind has been working overtime on these photos. Molly's right – I do have a habit of complicating simple things but I don't think the photos are just family snaps, which of course they are. Am I making sense? You see, Leonard, there are loads of these photos but they suddenly stop and I don't know why. I think something bad happened to the family and I need to find out what it was. It's just that I have this very strong feeling about it all. Call it an instinct if you like.

Have you ever heard stories about the way animals and birds behave before a disaster strikes? Do you remember the tsunami of 2004? Apparently, hours before it struck Sri Lanka all the animals in this wildlife park near the coast moved to higher ground and none of them died. They knew something was going to happen. I once read about a dam disaster in Italy that flooded some villages killing hundreds of people and after the disaster survivors spoke about the silence of the birds before the dam broke.

I've got the same eerie silence with these photos – like a tumbleweed moment. They stop around the 1970s not because there's a missing box of photos. There just aren't any more photos. I looked through all the images and just felt that there was a dreadful finality about that box, which meant that the Barker family just stopped taking snaps. I don't know why I know this and you'll probably think that I'm crazy. I don't know why it happened, this sudden halt in a lifetime of taking photos. It would be like an art gallery devoted to Vincent's paintings but missing the ones from Arles, Saint Rémy and Auvers, all those paintings that catalogue the state of his mind and his art towards the end of his life. Without those paintings, it would be as if Vincent's life had been cut short, a life's work somehow short-changed. This is how I feel about the Barkers.

I don't know anything about the family except for the photos. Mr Barker was a very private sort of person; we would speak occasionally but he didn't reveal much about himself and he never spoke about the past, which frankly is what most old people like to talk about all the time. I just feel that there are so many unanswered questions. Did the son leave home? Did he get married to the mini-skirted girl? Did they have kids? Was there a huge bust-up within the family and taking photos after that would just be like creating bad memories, permanent reminders of a huge family rift. So Mr and Mrs Barker just became resigned to growing old gracefully, sitting in their garden sipping afternoon tea until Mrs Barker gradually declined, leaving Mr Barker to face old age alone. That's a rather gloomy image, isn't it?

I know that Molly's right about Mr Barker being nothing to me. But the photos keep gnawing away at my brain. I keep seeing them in a sequence like in some old Hollywood film when the pages of a calendar are being torn off to mark the passing of time. The photos tell a story but it's like watching a television drama with the sound turned off. There's no narrative to help you to fully understand the story, just a series of images: boy, horse, soldier, wedding, baby, bucket and spade, pedal car, new house, new car, another new car, MG Midget. What did that neighbour say? No living relative… No living relative. A devoted father and mother who take hundreds of photos of each other and especially of their son would only stop doing this if some terrible event intervened.

Wait a minute, Leonard. I may have got it. The little boy in the pedal car, the teenager who looks up from his homework in a room whose walls are covered with pictures of racing cars and drivers, the young man whose girl friend adorns his sports car. What if the Barkers lost their son? Maybe the MG car was a clue. Maybe they lost him in a car accident and never took any more photos. That's got to be a possibility, Leonard. Do you think it's a possibility?

CHAPTER 2

Harry had finished mowing the lawns, front and back, and was now gasping for a cup of tea, which Molly, ever aware of his habits, would have waiting for him. Having stowed the mower back in the garage, after carefully wiping and oiling the blades, he took off his gardening shoes and entered the kitchen. But no Molly and, more disappointingly, no tea. Harry went into the hall and was about to call up the stairs when Molly's disembodied voice called down to him.

'I'm up here. Come up.'

'Up where?'

'Harry, just come up.'

Harry climbed the stairs grumpily and on the landing saw that the attic was open and the loft ladder propped up.

'I'm in the attic. I want you to come up.'

'Molly, what are you doing up there?' Attics were not a woman's territory. They were a male domain, even if Harry rarely went up there. He puffed his way up the ladder and, as his head emerged into the loft space, he could see Molly seated on an old kitchen chair, another chair placed opposite and two cups of steaming tea on an upturned packing case.

'Molly, what's going on? What on earth...'

'Harry, sit down, drink your tea and listen to me. We've got a problem.'

Harry surveyed the attic. The joists looked all right, no sign of woodworm, no daylight coming in from the roof itself, so no slipped slates, no damp patches anywhere, no evidence of birds, rats or mice, and no illegal immigrants hiding out.

'Harry, the problem is not in the attic. The problem is us. And before you ask why we're up here, I'll tell you. Every time we talk about our problems, and that's once in a blue moon, you look for something to avoid the issue. You can't sit still, you walk around, you look for distractions – so I thought I'd try to talk to you up here where there's less to sidetrack you.'

Although Harry found the situation bizarre, he deemed it a good idea to go along with it for the moment. Molly had that steely look about her that brooked no argument and so he didn't think getting up and leaving the attic was advisable.

'What do you mean – problems? What problems?'

Molly took a sip of her tea and seemed to be composing herself. The atmosphere in the attic was heavy with the smell of bone-dry trusses and roofing felt. Harry fidgeted uncomfortably on his chair as the trapped air wrapped itself around him. He hoped that whatever Molly had to say to him would be short and sweet because he could feel beads of sweat forming on the back of his neck. He caught a glimpse of a pile of dusty LPs in the corner behind Molly. Joni Mitchell's 'Blue' was on top and he wondered if the old Dansette record player next to the pile still worked because he hadn't heard the album in ages. *Maybe I could run an extension up here and play some of the old stuff. I wonder if I could pull up the loft ladder while I'm up here so that no one disturbs me.*

'Harry! Look at me when I'm trying to talk to you!' Molly took a deep, sighing breath. 'No, I'm not going to lose my cool. I'm going to keep calm. Harry, this is very important. I've got something to say to you and I want to know what you think. But first, let me say what I've got to say and please, please, don't interrupt.'

Harry sat motionless before his wife, like a small boy seated on the naughty step.

'The first thing I want to say... is that I still love you. I know you don't like statements of affection but I need to tell you. I love you. I think I loved you from the moment I caught sight of you, even before we actually spoke to each other. I remember the first time I ever saw you at that Moody Blues gig. You were with a couple of mates and you walked to your seat in a stooped sort of way as if you didn't think you should be there. Your arms and legs seemed to be quarreling with each other as you walked. You turned around self-consciously as you took your seat and I saw your face. And I knew at that moment that I wanted to get to know you.

'At the end of the gig, I thought you were going to speak to me but I think you were too shy and then you forgot your scarf. You looked so embarrassed. The next day I saw you going into the students' union and I decided to miss my lecture and follow you in. I sat near you so that you might notice me. But if you hadn't, I was determined to talk to you anyway. But you did come over, and that as we both know was that.'

Harry made to say something but Molly hushed him with her hand.

'I loved the times we spent together at uni. Every thing we did together, however silly or mundane, was an adventure. I loved your wacky slant on the world, the crazy things you used to say, your naivety, your kindness... but above all I loved *you*, the being that was you, the entity that was my Harry.

'And I know that life changes you, work changes you, having children changes you... I know that we can't be the people we were back then. But, Harry, where have *we* gone? You don't seem to want to talk to me any more; you're always busy doing something on your own. We don't go anywhere together. We don't actually live together any more. We just co-exist, rattling around in this house. And wherever I am, whenever I'd really like to be with you, to tell you about my day, to hear what you've been up to, you're never there because you're in the next room. If I could sum up what you've become, what our life has become, that says it all. You're in the next room, Harry, never with me. You're in the next room. And I don't want to go on like this for the rest of our lives.'

Molly paused and looked straight at Harry, indicating that it was now his turn to say something.

'It was Chicken Shack.'

'What?'

'Chicken Shack. The first time we saw each other, Chicken Shack were playing, not the Moody Blues.'

Dear Leonard,

I'm getting worried about Molly. She dragged up me to the attic this morning for a talk. I mean, the attic of all places. She talked about when we first met and at first I wondered if this might be the onset of Alzheimer's. Don't people with dementia start regressing to the past? She talked about other stuff, too – mainly us. It's always 'us'. 'Harry, we need to talk about *us*'. I know I'm not the best when it comes down to the 'us' conversation but I listened. I really did. But when it came for me to say something, she just flipped. I thought she was going to throw her tea at me. She stormed off downstairs and then I heard the front door slam and her car driving off.

She didn't come back till late afternoon. Turns out she went to my daughter's. That's what women do, don't they? When there's an emotional outburst, they seek each other out. It's some kind of herding instinct. We ate dinner in silence. I think she was angling for me to say sorry but it wasn't me who stormed out, was it? Maybe I should have said something. I don't like there to be an atmosphere.

What would you have done in the situation? You've had your tangled moments with the opposite sex. You talk about women most of the time. There was a time when Molly and I talked. We used to talk a lot actually – about anything, about everything. There was a time when we'd talk the world to sleep. But something got lost along the way. We used to have a switch that automatically clicked on when we were together, so that we became this single being rather than two separate parts. We could be doing different things but as long as we were together we felt part of a whole. Now we're just in a hole and we're falling ever further down it, into a fathomless black pit. What happened to us, Leonard? What changes people? When we first met we were pretty purposeless in everything we did, I must admit, but it didn't matter because we were young and in love. But why is that time like some lonely, forgotten place now? I'd give anything to recapture just a moment of that time but I've forgotten how. We all grow old but is it ordained that we must grow apart from the ones we love?

CHAPTER 3

Harry was sitting nervously on the sofa with Billy in his arms. He could not have looked more uncomfortable if someone had asked him to mind a baby gorilla while they popped to the shops.

'Are you sure his rash has gone? He looks a bit peaky to me.'

Hazel emerged briskly from the kitchen of the small flat with a cup of coffee in one hand and a bright blue beaker in the other. The purposeful way in which she carried herself owed much to her mother's traits. She had also inherited Molly's slight frame and stature. Her features, however, were unmistakeably those of her father, a cause of much teenage angst when glued in front of the mirror getting ready for the school disco but now a cross she bore with resigned acceptance. She placed the coffee cup in front of Harry and held out the beaker.

'Billy gets anxious with strangers but he'll be all right when he gets to know you. Here, give him this.'

Harry did not rise to the bait but looked for a third arm with which to execute the task of feeding Billy his drink.

'Let him hold it himself. He's not a baby.'

Billy took hold of the beaker in both hands and like a seasoned veteran began to guzzle contentedly, his eyes still appraising the man who was holding him at arm's length.

'Right, Mum said you had a leaky tap. Lead me to the patient and be on hand to mop my brow. This could be tricky'

Harry rose and plonked Billy unceremoniously into his daughter's arms.

'I'm sorry, Dad, but the tap was a ruse to get you over here. I wanted a chat with you without Mum knowing.'

Harry took a deep breath. What was it with the women in his life, always wanting to 'talk'? Why did Hazel need to take up the baton? Why couldn't people just get on with their lives? He didn't feel the need to 'talk' with anyone. And what did Hazel have to say to him? He'd had the husband-wife talk with Molly. Was Hazel going to do the father-daughter talk? Harry didn't think he'd been a great father. But he'd stayed the course when plenty of other dads had not reached the first hurdle, or came a cropper at the water jump. He hadn't lead the field from start to finish or broken any records but he thought he'd achieved a personal best in providing a good home and the comfort blanket of a loving, secure upbringing. So many of Hazel's friends had lost a parent to divorce or separation. Harry had done his bit, he thought, to guide his daughter through the choppy waters of adolescence and to help her scale the heights of higher education. Hazel was now a mature, married woman in her early thirties, with a baby and a husband with prospects.

Admittedly, Harry hadn't taken to Hazel's husband when he first met him. Ian was a self-assured young man with a promising career in pharmaceuticals. He was also charming – a word that Molly immediately ascribed to him when Hazel brought him home for the first time. Ian had complimented Molly on her dress, her cooking, the table setting, her roses, indeed everything. What a charming young man, Molly had said afterwards. What charming manners. Hasn't he got a winning smile, Harry?

Harry did not agree. Charm was an unguent of little importance to him. The two men had little in common. On one occasion, Molly and Hazel despatched the two of them to the pub while they looked at wedding dresses in magazines. Ian tried his best to find a conversation opener but none had legs and so they spent an agonising two hours staring into space.

But Harry began to warm to Ian when he announced that his parents wanted to go halves on the wedding and he hoped that Harry wouldn't be offended by their generous offer. Harry wasn't. From that point on their relationship, while never familial, improved to the level of an entente cordiale.

Billy had fallen asleep on Hazel's shoulder, the beaker still attached. She gently carried him upstairs for his midday nap. When she returned her father was seated stiffly in an armchair like an expectant interviewee.

'I wanted to say first that it's so nice having you come round, Dad, even if I have to use subterfuge.'

Harry remained silent. When was the 'talk' going to start?

'You'll probably think that I'm sticking my nose in where it doesn't belong but I'm going to anyway. It's just that Mum doesn't seem to be her normal self these days. She's usually very upbeat about things but I think she's lost her sparkle of late. I don't know why'

As he listened to his daughter Harry had a perplexed look on his face as if he was struggling to grasp the language in which he was being addressed.

'I know that when a couple retire it can take some re-adjusting, especially when you're under each other's feet all day. You two are on your own, rattling around in that big house. I think Mum would appreciate a bit of a change to her routine, you know, getting out a bit more – maybe a drive somewhere, a visit to the theatre or a meal out once in a while. What do you think?'

31

Harry pondered the question. This seemed to be quite a non-threatening 'talk' and replete with solutions.

'I don't mind Mum going for a drive. I've got plenty to do at home and she can go to the theatre whenever she…'

'Dad! With you! Mum wants to do things with you.'

'Oh, she's never said anything.'

'She's probably hinted at it but perhaps you didn't pick it up on your radar. Men often have that problem.'

And, thought Harry, women can never say what they mean. Always the scenic route rather than straight up the A470.

'So what do you think, Dad? You could take her for a meal tomorrow. She'd love it and it would be a lovely surprise. She's mentioned that new Italian place on Wellfield Road. It got a really good write-up in the Echo.'

'Can't.'

'Can't?'

'Thursday's my local history meeting and it's the AGM.'

Hazel composed herself. She wasn't going to storm out of her own flat.

'Dad, do you remember when I was a little girl and I got stuck up the tree in our old house? I was about seven, I think. Mum was visiting grandma for the day or something. Chris would have been four and he was going through that irritating phase – did he ever stop? - always spoiling whatever I was doing. I was having a dolls' tea party on the back lawn and he just ran over and kicked them everywhere. I picked up the nearest thing and threw it at him. But it was one of his dinky cars and it hit him in the mouth. His lip seemed to explode and there was blood everywhere. Of course, he started squealing like a stuck pig and I just panicked. I raced down the garden and climbed up the tree – I don't know how I got up there – and waited for the inevitable.'

'I remember all that but why are you bringing it up now?'

'Just wait, Dad. Eventually, you came down to the tree with Chris in tow and looked up at me. You'd mopped him up and his lip wasn't bleeding any more. I was rather perilously perched on this branch and you must have been anxious that I'd fall. But you just spoke calmly and told me that there was nothing to worry about. Chris had told you everything and, though I was wrong to have retaliated, it was just an accident. You said that Chris was okay and I should just climb down. I remember that Chris was crying, not because of his lip but because he was afraid I'd fall. I don't know why but I said I was going to stay up the tree, even though I was feeling pretty scared by now. I could see all our neighbours watching me from their gardens. I could be very stubborn – don't know where I got that trait from.'

Harry moved uncomfortably in his chair.

'Anyway, you asked me when I intended to come down and I said that I was going stay there forever. Then you said, "Oh, so you're going to be another Simeon Stylites, are you?" The name intrigued me straightaway and I asked who he was. You said that if I came down you'd tell me his story and, of course, I knew that I would have to because I was always a sucker for new information and you knew this.

'So, you got the ladder and put it against the branch I was sitting on. You couldn't put it as close as you'd like because the weight of it might have toppled me. You told me to shuffle along on my bottom and you would grab hold of me when I was close enough. I was petrified by now because the branch was shaking and so

33

was I but I did what you said and finally you took hold of me. I wrapped my arms and legs around you like a baby baboon on its mother's back and slowly you climbed down the ladder. I remember the neighbours all cheered when we were safely on the ground. That evening Chris and I had our bath and he went straight to bed because he was so flaked out by the day's events. But we went downstairs and you gave me milk and biscuits – something Mum never allowed before bedtime – and you told me all about Simeon Stylites, about how he spent 40 years living in the desert on top of a pillar…'

'37 actually…'

'Dad, the exact time period's irrelevant. He spent all that time up a pole to prove how holy he was.'

'That's right but I don't get the point of what you're trying to say.'

'The point is that you're becoming the Simeon Stylites of this family. You're up a metaphorical pole – I won't tell you where it's stuck – because you seem to prefer isolation to any form of contact, physical or emotional, with us, your family. You never want to see Ian and me on our own turf and when we visit you and Mum you always seem to have a little job that can't be left. Ian finds you very standoffish. And I know he's a bit in your face at times but he has a lot of respect for you. And as for Billy, you hardly know him. We wouldn't want him growing up thinking he only has one granddad. You live in the same house as Mum but from what I gather you're a bit of a hermit.'

Ah, thought Harry, this is the mother-daughter conspiracy. This is what they talked about when Molly stormed off.

'We're all worried about you, Dad.'

Dear Leonard,

So there we have it. My wife and daughter have ganged up on me. I have been tried in my absence and convicted of crimes against family. I am guilty of not being able to read my wife's inner thoughts and understand her need for more companionship and affection. I have neglected my fatherly duties to my daughter and her child, and I am too aloof towards her husband. I've probably offended my son, too. I can see myself standing in a sort of police line-up along which Christopher is slowly walking, scrutinising our faces. When it's done, he will be asked *Can you see your father amongst them?* and he will reply with a catch in his voice *No, he's not there but if he was I wouldn't recognise him. He was always a stranger to me anyway.* You think they all have a point, don't you Leonard? I can sense it. You think I'm being over-sensitive because I'm uncomfortable with the truth. That's your trouble, Leonard. You're like a searchlight pointed at the human condition, penetrating even the darkest corners.

The tragedy is that even when I was a kid I felt like an outsider in my own home. When you were growing up, did you ever feel out touch with your family and your surroundings, that somehow you just didn't belong and that you'd been parachuted into an environment that was totally alien to your sensitivities? You must know the stories in folklore about changelings, babies who were taken away by fairies and replaced by children who were strangers in their new family. I felt like a changeling in my family because I was totally out of kilter with my parents and with my elder sister. We had nothing in common. From an early age, I stood out as different. I was reading newspapers before my sister picked up her first Janet and John book. I drove my parents mad with my continuous questions about everything under the sun. When I was old enough to start musing on the obvious differences between them and me, I actually thought that there must have been a mix-up in the hospital when I was born or that I had been adopted. I dismissed the second theory pretty quickly because why would my parents adopt me when they already had an older child? But the hospital mix-up seemed credible enough. Two babies born on the same day but their identities swapped by mistake. I had visions of a middle-class family in Bideford forever wondering why their son was an inarticulate yokel built like a Sherman tank. Physically, I was nothing like my parents. My mother was a little on the heavy side but my father was tall and burly with biceps that could crush walnuts. My sister looked like an East German shot-putter. And me? I was thin and weedy and, in spite of my poor mother's attempts to bulk me up with pies and puddings, I was still like a breath of wind.

I think I could have coped with being the changeling in my family but starting school only emphasised my uniqueness. My first teacher wouldn't accept that I could read, so I had to plough through the same reading books as everyone else. I played along and did what I was told but I would find different books to read on the bookshelves that lined the corridor. In the end, the school just let me carry on because I was no trouble and I fulfilled a valuable role whenever a narrator was required for a school production.

But the worst aspect of school life was the other kids. They sniffed me out from the start. I was the weakling in the pack and their instincts were feral. Being bullied was part and parcel of being an intelligent, sensitive and whey-faced boy in the midst of a multitude of horny-handed sons of the soil – a slap here, a dig in the ribs there and the taunts of 'you should have been a girl.' I can't say I was brutalised by them, many children have suffered worse, but I was always on my guard and learned to anticipate situations where I might become the victim. My primary school days made me wary of others. I was never one of the gang. I was afraid to get too close to people because any encounter could easily end in, well, anything you could imagine, and usually worse.

CHAPTER 4

Harry was patrolling the Impressionists' collection on the first floor of the art gallery in the National Museum of Wales. It was 11.00am and outside the museum the overcast skies weighed down heavily upon Cathays Park, giving the sun no chance to illuminate the vast acreage of Portland stone that was such a feature of Cardiff's civic centre. Only a few desultory visitors were viewing the collection. Harry would occasionally sidle up to them in the hope that they might ask him something – anything – but they weren't biting. Harry had been in the job for about a month and he was feeling a little disheartened. He knew he was fortunate to be allocated to paintings but, to be fair, he had impressed the panel at his interview. 'You have a commendable knowledge of art history, Mr Dymond'. Commendable. He rolled the word around his mind. But wasted if no one asks me anything, he thought.

Harry knew that he had other duties to perform other than being a fountain of knowledge to interested visitors. But that was the main reason he applied for the part-time post of museum attendant – to impart knowledge, to inform, to clarify, to enlighten. Enlighten – that was his task. Anyone could walk about the galleries watching out for potential trouble – noisy schoolchildren, the occasional dosser coming in out of the cold, an old lady having a fainting fit. But Harry could do so much more, if only someone would care to seek out the truth and wisdom he could impart.

Here for example was one of Monet's paintings of Rouen cathedral. Harry would have taken the visitor as closely as possible to the painting so that the cathedral's façade appeared as merely a rosy blur. Then he would have told the visitor to continue looking but to move back slowly, very slowly, until the image reveals itself in all its glory. Harry would then have launched into detail about Monet's passion for painting the effects of light under different conditions, hence the series of cathedral paintings produced over time from a single vantage point. But at this moment it was Harry alone who was appreciating this masterpiece. In fact, he was so engrossed in the painting that he didn't notice his colleague Meera alongside him and he jumped when she spoke.

'Elaine says she would like a quick word with you at the end of your shift'

'Did she say what about?' Harry was always wary about what a 'quick' word might entail.

'She didn't say but she seemed fine. It's probably something and nothing.'

Harry finished his shift and made his way to his supervisor's office. Elaine was a round-faced fifty-something whose fuller figure seemed to be in a constant state of war with her uniform and it was the uniform that was losing the battle. As Harry sat nervously opposite her, he struggled to keep his eyes from straying towards her enormous bosoms, as they rested their weight on the desk top before renewing their struggle to burst out of the white shirt that was bravely trying to contain them.

'Thanks for coming up. I won't keep you long because I know you'll be wanting to get home. I just wanted to see how things were going your end. You know, you've been here a month now.'

Harry could not discern exactly what was being asked of him. The phrase 'to see how things were going your end' was imprecise and he'd actually been in the museum's employment for 34 days. Best to ask a question, he thought.

'Is there a problem?'

'No, I just wanted to know if you're enjoying the work and whether you feel that you have settled in. Are the hours that we agreed working out for you?'

Harry relaxed a little and answered each question in the affirmative although in truth he was struggling to gel with his colleagues. They were polite enough and initially very helpful but once the first few days were over he could see the same pattern emerging. They were already finding him rather aloof and standoffish and he only had himself to blame if they were reacting as others had done before. Harry had never found the relaxed camaraderie of the workplace a comfortable atmosphere and it looked like he was going to have to endure the same experience again.

'Good. Pleased to hear it,' said Elaine and then after a rather long pause, 'Perhaps I have one suggestion for you, Harry, which I hope you won't mind me mentioning.'

Wait for it, thought Harry, here it comes.

'I observed you yesterday in one of the galleries. Not snooping I can assure you. Just passing through. You looked a trifle … uneasy, perhaps a little stiff and awkward and, dare I say it …stern. Now we don't want our visitors to feel intimidated by our attendants, do we? What I'm saying is, try to be a bit more relaxed and visitors will interact with you if they find you approachable. Do you get my drift?'

Harry felt crestfallen. Wasn't he trying to do his best? How he envied those people who just slipped so easily into the social intercourse of life. Why couldn't he find the key? He thought he should say something to Elaine but couldn't find the words.

'I'm sorry…'he began.

'Look, Harry, there's no need to apologise. I've probably overstated the case but I just want you to get the most out of your work. You've made a good start but maybe you're trying a bit too hard. Remember: relax and enjoy.'

Dear Leonard,

I suppose I shouldn't read so much into my line manager's little 'chat' because I actually like where I work, even though I'm struggling to win my colleagues' acceptance. When I was offered the job after the interview, it was like asking a small boy if he'd like to look after the sweetshop. When I walk into the galleries at the start of each shift, I feel lifted out of my mundane self and for those few precious hours my anxieties fall away. I never tire of looking at the artworks on display and they give me a kind of consolation I can find nowhere else.

I remember how I first become fascinated by art. I was in my final year of primary school and I had just sat my 11-plus examination, which was hopefully my passport to the grammar school. For most of my classmates the 11-plus was nothing to worry about – you either passed it or you didn't. But for me it meant everything. I think you'll gather by now that I wasn't a popular boy at school; I was tolerated rather than liked. For one thing I was hopeless at sport and particularly football, an activity that carried more weight amongst the boys of my age than anything else. Devon was a county that could boast only three lower division league football clubs but that didn't deter a grubby band of Jimmy Greaves acolytes from my class at Great Torrington Junior School, who spent every break time kicking nine bells out of a battered leather football. I got used to being the last one picked for football. I would end up standing somewhere in defence, usually blocking the goalie's view and aiming the odd miss-kick when the ball came in my direction. If I had been gifted with any silky skills, I would still have struggled to display them because my brawny classmates favoured a rather uncompromising approach to tackling and inevitably I would be painfully brushed aside or clattered to the ground.

I was an avid reader of the Jennings books – they were very popular in those days - and I loved burying myself in world of Linbury Court School. I knew it was all fiction but I was so aware of how incongruous I was amongst my peers. The grammar school had to be better. My extensive knowledge and my voracious appetite for ever more information held no sway with my classmates but in the grammar school I dreamed of finding boys like me, maybe even just one friend who would be Darbishire to my Jennings.

One Saturday, as I sat listening to Uncle Mac on the radio, my mother came back from the shops and dropped a magazine in my lap.

'Thought you might like this,' she said as she unpacked her shopping bag. 'It's got your name written all over it.'

It was a magazine I'd seen in a newsagent's in Bideford but to which my pocket money never stretched, a children's magazine full of illustrated articles on every subject under the sun – history, geography, science, nature, literature and music.

'I've ordered it for you every week. You've always got your head in a book anyway and if…when you pass for the grammar school, it'll help you with your studies, I'm sure. Do you like the look of it?'

Of course I liked it but my face gave me away.

'Don't worry. We can afford it. I've got a new cleaning job in Bideford, a bachelor chap, and he wants me to do his laundry, too. So, I'll have a bit of spare cash to go on nice things. But don't tell you dad, will you?'

And so every Saturday thereafter, I would be waiting like Pavlov's dog for the tinny clunk of the letterbox and the arrival of the magazine that would nourish my hunger for knowledge. I would immediately read it from cover to cover and, with my father normally working on a Saturday morning, my mother would leave me in peace. I absorbed information like a sponge and no article lost my attention, even those on subjects like science or nature, which I knew I wouldn't pursue in the future. But what really stirred my passions were the articles on famous artists, complete with illustrations of their work. The only art we had in my house was a smoke-stained copy of The Fighting Temeraire, which hung above the fireplace. I had heard of artists by name – Rembrandt, Picasso and Constable – but I had no concept of their particular artworks or style, and only a hazy chronology of the eras in which they lived. But now each week a new painter or sculptor joined the pantheon of artists that began to inhabit my mind. I loved the art displayed in the magazine each week but I was also fascinated by the stories about how these works were created: Michelangelo painting on vertiginous scaffolding for four years to complete the ceiling of the Sistine Chapel, Leonardo employing six musicians to keep Lisa Gheradini happy while he captured that almost imperceptible smile, Turner strapped to the mast of a storm-tossed sailing ship in order to experience a tempest at first hand and Picasso's anger expressed in a masterpiece of abstraction to convey the horror of the bombing of Guernica. I had no ambitions myself to emulate the artists who now filled my mind. I knew my drawing skills were 'woefully weak' (as my school report attested) but it didn't matter. I had gained entry into a world of light, shade and colour where the imagination of geniuses ran riot. In works of art I found a level of truth and permanence that did not exist in my everyday life. I realise now why art was so important to me. I was entering an adolescent world of change and responsibility that frankly scared me to death, but in appreciating art I could cling on to images that remained fixed and absolute, that had no need to change since they were an embodiment of immutable perfection. Millais's Ophelia was a prime example: her flower-strewn body gracefully sinking beneath the water, forever caught in the agonising bliss of a slow death by drowning. The artifice of the painting did not matter and the knowledge that Elizabeth Siddons had lain for hours in a tin bath with only candles underneath in a vain attempt to keep the water warm only gave an added piquancy to my enjoyment of this Pre-Raphaelite masterpiece.

Sorry, Leonard, I'm rambling a bit, aren't I? I'm afraid I get carried away on the subject. I'll speak to you again.

CHAPTER 5

The following Saturday Harry and Molly's son, Christopher, came for the day. There were only two reasons for a filial visit – he was either between girlfriends or his washing machine was on the blink again. The laundry bag told its story. A bizarre transaction always took place on these occasions. He would bring his laundry, which his mother would dutifully wash and iron, and when he left both parents would give him £20 surreptitiously. 'Don't tell your mother.' 'Don't tell your father.'

Father and son sat watching the football while Molly ironed in the kitchen. At half time Harry told Chris about Mr Barker's photos. Chris listened to his father's story indulgently; he was a training to be a legal executive and he felt that his father's theory needed the application of his keen legal brain.

'I think you're ignoring a number of possibilities here, Dad. Mr Barker's son could have emigrated and then lost touch with his parents. Perhaps he joined the army and got killed in Northern Ireland. Or maybe he embezzled some money and ended up in clink. You have no evidence that he died in a car crash. I think the theory of a mega family bust-up is the more likely.'

'I've gone off that idea,' said Harry. 'A major family argument seems a bit far-fetched now.'

'You quarrelled with Auntie Susan and you haven't spoken to her in years.'

'That's different and anyway she's the one in the wrong. She knows where I live if she decides to apologise.'

'You could do the noble thing and make the first call.'

'She started the row and she should finish it. Look, we're straying from the photos. Have you got any better theories?'

'Have you considered alien abduction?'

Harry wished that he had kept the photos to himself. He felt slightly foolish. His son clearly didn't see their significance.

The second half got underway and soon Chris was engrossed in the game. In his mind Harry looked again at the MG Midget with the girl stretched out on the bonnet. He had a feeling that the car held the answer and suddenly his next step was revealed to him.

The football match had finished but Chris was slow to leave. Harry was hoping that Molly wouldn't ask her son to stay for tea. After what seemed like an age Chris finally left, £40 richer. Harry immediately dashed upstairs to his son's bedroom as Molly called after him:

'Don't forget Dan and Julie are coming round later. You'll need to go out for beer. Get some nibbles while you're at it. And can you pick up the dry cleaning? If it's warm enough, we'll sit out in the conservatory. The patio could do with a hosing, by the way.'

Harry grunted a reply as he rushed into his son's old bedroom and took down the album from the wardrobe. He found the page and the photo he was looking for – the girl on the bonnet of the son's car. He took in the scene. It was a bright summer's day and the roses scrambling up the side of the house were in full bloom. The MG was parked on the drive and the only person in the picture was the girl. Harry could see that it was late afternoon because the person behind the camera – most likely the son – cast a long shadow right up to the wheel arches of the car. Harry focussed on the girl, her pose provocative but ironic, her blonde hair flowing loosely, a tight sweater emphasising her bust, her skirt just preserving her modesty. Following her shapely leg from thigh to ankle, as it rested on the bonnet, Harry could see what he had missed before, clear as daylight, etched by the sun flooding from behind the camera – the car's number plate, JOE 679C.

~

Dan and Julie had the misfortune to be teachers still working in Harry's old school. This meant that the main topics of conversation at the meal revolved around what changes the new head had implemented, why they were bad changes, why the staff were 'up in arms' about the said changes and how teachers and teaching were no longer appreciated.

'You're lucky, Harry. You got out at the right time.'

I got out because I no longer wanted to have conversations like this, thought Harry, but thank you, Dan, for giving me the vicarious pleasure of being back in the staff room.

Harry noticed that Molly was somewhat testy towards him but he assumed that it was because he had forgotten to pick up the dry cleaning, his mind being distracted by the revelation of the number plate. He was desperate to check the registration number on the computer. He didn't know what he wanted to check but he knew that the computer was the next step.

'Are you off to France in the near future?' asked Julie, glancing at the watercolour of a cottage on the dining room wall. 'Such a pretty place you've got,' - then reading the title in her best French accent - 'Pont Caramel.'

'It's *Camarel*,' Harry corrected. 'It's not a chocolate from a Black Magic box.'

Casting a withering glance in Harry's direction, Molly cut in:

48

'We're going over in a week or two to shut it down for the winter. You two must come over with us some time. It's lovely in the spring.'

Harry nearly choked on his corn-fed chicken breast wrapped in pancetta.

~

It was the following morning before Harry could have some time to himself. Molly was downstairs preparing Sunday lunch and he'd promised to peel the potatoes. The computer took ages to boot up and Harry's stomach tightened as he waited. When he finally got on the internet, it didn't take him long to find sites about MG Midgets. There were enthusiasts all over the world. But Harry didn't want to know that the Midget was based on the Austin Healey Sprite or that at some point in the car's history its quarter-elliptic leaf springs had been replaced with semi-elliptic ones.

The more he refined his search, the more information he got. He could hear kitchen doors slamming downstairs, a sure sign that Molly was getting mad at his absence. He googled one more time and the ninth entry on the page offered him a lost and found site that traced the history of MG models and marques. He quickly punched in the car's registration number, logged off and ran downstairs. The noise and steam issuing from the kitchen told him that Molly was venting her spleen on the vegetables but he sauntered in as if nothing was wrong:

'Sorry, computer's on the blink again. Took an age to get going but I think I've fixed it now. Right, where's those spuds?'

Dear Leonard,

I think I'm on to something with the car, now that I've found the registration number. I'm sure there's someone out there who has some information about it. A number plate with a person's name on it is valuable. People will pay a lot for a personalised plate, so I'm pretty sure it would have survived even if the car ended up scrapped. We'll just have to wait, won't we?

Molly's still tetchy with me by the way. It seems I was rude to our friend Julie at dinner the other evening. People are so sensitive, aren't they? And, of course, teachers are even worse and as an ex-teacher I should know. Teachers have very high opinions of themselves, you know, and I used to be the same. It's as if God created all the occupations in the world and then on the Sabbath day he created teachers, the chosen ones. Have you ever seen those rear number plates that say 'If you can read this, thank a teacher'? What tosh! I want to say 'If you can read this, you've only got a reading age of a six year old, so blame a teacher.' Why do they think they're so superior?

And, while I'm on the subject, there's a peculiar habit that teachers have when they're talking about other teachers. Instead of saying that in the past they worked together, they will say 'I *taught* with him at such-and-such school.' I *taught* with him, my arse! I mean to say, would an engineer say 'I engineered with him at Esso' or a computer programmer utter 'We programmed together at IBM.' It's because teachers think they're born, not made. They are called to this mystical higher place to be entrusted with that most precious of vocations, the education of young minds. I feel I ought to be speaking all this to you in hushed tones. And to think I was once admitted to this self-same priesthood, to practise the hallowed rites of guiding God's children to the Promised Land. And there's another thing. Do you know that when I taught, I mean *worked* as a teacher, we used to get official guidance on the latest teaching methodology and these documents that were endlessly spewed out at us would speak not of ways to teach kids some new stuff but would use terms like 'learning gateways' and 'learning portals'. So you can see that even the administrators believe the same guff.

Sorry, Leonard, I'd better get off my soapbox and, yes, I have had a drink or three this evening. This is Molly's choir evening and I know I'll get that look of hers when she returns but there was a bottle calling to me from the wine rack and I can resist everything except Tempranillo, so there.

CHAPTER 6

Harry was having a better morning. Molly had actually exchanged a few words with him at breakfast before she left for work. She had a part-time job as a receptionist at a local optician. It didn't pay well but she wasn't rushed and it was only three mornings a week. And more importantly it got her out of the house.

'What are you up to today?' she asked, glancing at her watch, as she put her cereal bowl in the dishwasher.

Harry wasn't sure about the phrasing of the question. It suggested furtiveness and secrecy.

'Nothing special. I might tidy up the garage while you're out.'

'Yes, I noticed your paint tins weren't in alphabetical order,' she said under her breath and then 'Jenny came into the shop yesterday. She was picking up some new contact lenses. She said in passing that Bill and the others miss you in the quiz. She may have meant that they're not winning any more since you gave it up. Why did you stop going? You love quizzes. You're always glued to Eggheads.'

Harry knew that there was a hidden agenda in Molly's words but he couldn't quite put his finger on it. Did she want him out of the house on a Thursday?

'If you must know,' he said, 'I would rather be in a locked room with Ann Widdecombe and Piers Morgan than go to another quiz with that lot. Three of them are stone deaf, two are as blind as bats and three of them possess the brain cells of a retarded sloth – and there were only five of us in the team.'

'Harry, do you think that occasionally you might be a tad intolerant towards you fellow human beings?'

'Intolerant? The last time I went to the quiz, we were on a tie-break for a jackpot of £70; the first team to get the correct answer would win the lot. The question asked for the name of Napoleon's horse at the Battle of Waterloo. Easy but it was like the deaf version of Chinese whispers. I said Marengo but Bob thought I'd said Murano and delighted in telling me that it was the Venetian island where they made glass. Mike overheard him but thought he'd said Mourinho, the football manager, and finally Will wrote down Merino, rushed up with his answer and, of course, it was wrong. Napoleon's horse had turned into a breed of sheep.'

'Well, it's up to you but, according to Jenny, they've got a new quizmaster and he's a big improvement on the last one. What did you call him – the tother who had left hith brain on the buth – I believe he may have had a slight lisp? Anyway, have fun in the garage,' she said, as she gathered up her keys and left the kitchen.

Harry was left feeling a little confused at what seemed like forced normality on Molly's part. But at least they were talking again.

Harry did not tidy up the garage. It was pristine as was its wont, with every implement neatly hung on regimented hooks and every nail and screw accounted for. Molly rarely entered the garage for fear her movement would disturb its karma and cause hoes and spades to fly through the air, while number 6 and number 8 screws would explode from their allotted boxes and have their evil way with offcuts of MDF. No, Harry went up into the loft. The Dansette record player was beckoning him. He first tested it downstairs and found to his delight that it still worked. With drill, cable and toolbox carried up into the attic, he carefully measured from the centre of the floor and, finding the exact spot he wanted, drilled through the plasterboard.

A few trips up and down the ladder confirmed that he had made a hole inside the built-in wardrobe of the spare room and it did not take him long to feed the cable through the hole, wire it to a plug and connect it to the socket next to the wardrobe. A double socket on the other end of the cable in the attic completed the task. He plugged in the Dansette and glanced through the LP sleeves in the pile. They exuded a sensation of nostalgia bottled up for the past forty years: James Taylor, Steeleye Span. What treasures, thought Harry. But it was Joni Mitchell whom he carefully extracted from her blue sleeve and placed gently on the turntable. The record crackled into life in all its tinny sweetness:

All I really, really want our lo-ve to do-oo
Is to bring out the best in me and in you-ou too.

As Joni trilled away, Harry tidied up, clearing the attic of his tools and the wardrobe of any dust. Conscious that Molly would return by lunchtime, he decided to shut up the loft and leave Joni to another day. In the meantime, he would check his email. His inbox was full of the usual dross and he was about to delete the lot and shut the computer down when he saw that he had missed an email from the night before. It had the briefest of messages: 'Have some information about JOE 679C.' Harry dialled the phone number given, which was local, and as it was answered he could hear in the background the sound of a radio punctuated by the tell-tale noises of a busy workshop.

'I bought the car about 15 years ago, maybe more. Old guy, it was. Been in his garage for years. Must have been a lovely car in its day but it was wrecked. Been in a crash, see; front caved in; parts seized up. Felt sorry for the old chap. He was a bit, you know, he'd lost it. Trying to remember where he lived. Somewhere off Heathway, I seem to remember.'

Harry gave the address.

'That's it. Knew him, did you? The old guy mumbled something about his son being in the car and, of course, I saw the number plate. Thought to myself, too spooky, but I bought it anyway. I do up MGs in my spare time, for the American market mainly. They're mad on them over there. Got the money, see. Gave the old chap cash. Fair price, mind. Looked as if he could do with it. Doing him a favour, really, taking it away. What was the point of keeping that wreck in the garage for all that time? Beats me. In the end I didn't fully restore it. I sold it to a bloke in Cyncoed who was mad on cars and was looking for a project. We agreed a price and then when I delivered it and saw how big his house was, I wished I'd asked for double.'

Harry thanked the man and rang off. Suddenly he felt very tired.

Dear Leonard,

Well, the saga of the MG seems to be solved. The circle is closed as it were but I have to say Leonard that it gives me no satisfaction. My hunch has been proved correct but what it's revealed is a life more tragic than I'd thought. Mr Barker kept the wrecked car for over 20 years, a constant reminder of his son's untimely death. I now realise that when I found the old chap wandering in the street, he was looking for his son. He was looking for Joe.

The loss of a child in such circumstances must have been devastating for the old chap and he never came to terms with it. Even when he succumbed to dementia, the tragedy of Joe's passing still haunted him.

This whole business has made me think about Hazel and Christopher. They must be the same age as Joe when he got killed and it has made me think of what would happen if, you know. It's a morbid thought and of course they're in their prime but so was Joe. If you asked me whether I loved my children, I'd say of course I do. I'm bound to love them, aren't I? But I'd have to say that I've been a bit hopeless in showing them that I do and that's always been my trouble. Sometimes, Leonard, we can hurt the ones we love by things we say, harsh words spat out in anger; but I'm beginning to realise that things unsaid can also cause pain and I know I'm guilty of keeping my emotions under lock and key. Why do I do this? I don't like myself for doing this but I can't seem to break out of it.

CHAPTER 7

Harry was at a loose end. Molly was in work and had told him that she wouldn't be home for lunch. She was going shopping with a friend. Reading normally filled most gaps in his day but not today. The garden needed attention before winter arrived but it was pouring with rain and he'd already watched enough daytime television. The computer was an obvious last resort.

First, a quick check of his emails and what immediately caught his attention was an email from Molly.

Dear Harry,

After the debacle in the attic and since I am still determined to get through to you one way or another, I have decided to resort to email. Of course, you can delete this if you wish but I fancy that you will at least read it once before doing so. I think talking to you the other day was too sudden for you and maybe my approach was a little unbalanced. There is a problem with our relationship and it can't be brushed under the carpet and I'm sorry to say that the problem lies with you but I believe it does. However, for the sake of a fair and balanced approach I have made a list of your good and bad points (in no particular order), good points first:

1. You have been a good provider. I don't mean this in a patronising sense because I worked too when the children were older but you were never out of work. I know that your job was not very rewarding in later years and some men might have looked for a change. But you put us, the family, first and stuck at it. I think you may feel bitter about this and perhaps you felt that you were just there to keep the wolf from the door, having sacrificed a more promising career for just being a wage slave but all I can say is that I am proud of you for what you did and maybe I should have told you this more often.

2. You have been a good father. You may not think so and perhaps you could try a little harder now. Just

because Hazel and Christopher don't live with us any more doesn't mean they've ceased to be our children and especially *your* children. But when they were young, you did everything you could in spite of being stressed for most of the time. Sorry, back to work again. The thing I remember most is that you never contradicted me in front of the children. If I did get something wrong, like chastising them too severely, you always backed me, even though you might tell me afterwards. I think I was too dominant in the father-mother relationship and perhaps squeezed you out a bit. I can remember you coming home from work all whacked out and the kids all telling you what they'd done with mum that day and it must have seemed sometimes that you had nothing of worth to give them. But it's not true. You took them out to do the rough and tumble stuff that I hated and you were much better than I was at the moral bit. I think I was always too indulgent with them because I loved them too unconditionally. You gave them the moral compass that guided them into becoming good adults and you need to be reminded of that. Do you remember when Christopher dug up the bulbs that you had so carefully planted? I played hell with him when I found out but then I relented and told him I'd re-plant them and we wouldn't tell Daddy because he worked so hard and would be angry when he found out. If the bulbs didn't appear in the spring we could blame the frost. But when you went up to read him a bedtime story that night, he told you what he'd done because he knew that's what Daddy had taught him. I think that speaks volumes about the kind of dad you were.

3. You never leave the toilet seat up. This may seem trite but it is apparently endemic amongst most husbands and, perish the thought, some don't always flush.

4. You are a very good driver and have always got us to places on time. We have never missed a connection, never missed a flight or a ferry and I think in the past the kids and I have made light about your holiday planning, etc, even though perhaps you

stressed too much and tended to plan a holiday like the D-Day Landings. We must have seemed very uncooperative and I for one am sorry for this and I think we all could have been a bit more understanding.

5. You have been good in bed, I think. I know you may not like me commenting on this aspect of our life or perhaps you'd prefer me to say that you were a tiger in the bedroom. But I have never had anyone else to compare you with. But if a good lover is sensitive as well as the obvious, then you have been good. I'm sorry if I have been less responsive in recent years and I know women of a certain age can be pains in the neck but I still love your presence in bed and I wish we could re-ignite the flame as it were. Sorry about the cliché.

6. You never moaned about digging hair out of the plughole in the shower. It's a job I hated and when Hazel had long hair the shower was always getting blocked.

7. You are very good around the house and garden. Some husbands are hopeless with DIY, either doing nothing or attempting too much. You know your limits and have done more than most. When are you going to finish our bathroom? (Joke).

8. You always do the bins and recycling really well. I know I moan that you're a bit too meticulous about the recycling. You know, the planet will not shrivel up if I put a yoghurt carton in the wrong bin but you're right. If everybody followed your example then there'd be far less landfill.

9. You are very good with money. Perhaps I should have included this in point 2 but it's slightly different because apart from bringing the money in you have used it well. You know that this has never been my strong point and you have always taken on this burden. No bills go unpaid, you have invested well what little surplus we have and I have never had to worry about us getting in difficulties. If I handled our finances, all the paperwork would end up behind the clock and we'd end up in a debtor's prison. (Before

you correct me, I know such institutions no longer exist – but I've been reading *Little Dorrit*.)

10. You have always been faithful. An obvious thing to say, perhaps, but we know the consequences of infidelity amongst some of our friends. You have also never been flirtatious with other women or caused me to feel jealous, apart from lusting after Olivia Newton-John in the seventies. What did you see in her? I might have liked you flirting with other women. On second thoughts, I wouldn't and I'm glad that you didn't.

I was going to list your bad points now but maybe I'll leave that for another time because I think it's all too much to digest in one go. And it'll keep you guessing.
Love,
Molly

Dear Leonard,

Can you believe it? My wife has started to correspond with me by email. We live in the same house for goodness sake. What's happening here? I don't know why she has to list my good and bad points. It's a bit personal, isn't it, to think that you're being assessed by your wife on the standards of your behaviour. If I do something wrong is she going to score me like 'Strictly Come Dancing'? Will I get some marks for artistic merit?

The worse thing she could have commented on is my being a father. I've never felt comfortable about this. She says I was good at it but is she just saying that to make me feel better? I always felt that it wasn't the best time of my life. I'd been teaching for about seven years when Hazel came along. We were quite poor in those days even though we were both working when she was born. We'd taken on a big mortgage at the wrong time. Interest rates went soaring and we were running just to keep still. Right at the same time the head of the History department in my school retired – he'd been marking time for years and I was holding the department together - so I really thought that I would be filling his shoes. After all, I was second in the department by then and I thought that my promotion was a shoe-in. But this all coincided with a new headteacher who wanted to impress the governors. New broom and all that. He thought the history department was not dynamic enough. Dynamic, my foot. You try teaching the agrarian revolution of the 18th century to inner city teenagers. They thought Jethro Tull invented the seed drill while playing the flute standing on one leg. Okay, this is a bit strange to you but do you get the gist of what I'm saying?

Anyway, when the vacancy for head of department was announced, one of my colleagues in the department began to flex his muscles. He'd been teaching about four or five years, with a degree from Oxford no less and he was into historical methodology in a big way. History as a chronological narrative was out of the window. It was all about discovering history for yourself. Well, the kids in the lower seniors lapped it up. Nothing to actually learn and remember. No facts. No dates. They discovered history by looking at sources and drawing their own conclusions. Big wows! I did that as well but my approach was more of the established view, the body of knowledge already laid down. I mean I wasn't some kind of teaching dinosaur.

But this chap started to suck up to the new headteacher straightway. Maybe I should have done more to sell myself but I've never been good at self-promotion. I've always thought that your work should speak for itself but I suppose that's a bit naïve. Anyway, it turned out that the new headteacher had been to Oxford, too. Next thing I know, my colleague and the new head are bosom buddies and Mr-Down-With-The-Kids has applied for the vacancy. My vacancy! And, of course, he got it. He was younger than me and had less teaching experience, but he had the right credentials. When he got the job, he took me aside. 'No hard feelings, old chap. But we need to move this department into the 20th century and I'd like to think that you and I could really shake things up and make this a department to be proud of. Are you on board?' On board? I'd been tied to the ship's wheel for years and, if I do say so myself, navigating that department through pretty choppy waters, but that's not the point. The job should have been mine. I deserved it.

You think I'm rambling, don't you? The thing is, I couldn't work with the new head of department. And it wasn't sour grapes. He was too demanding. Not the workload, you understand but the changes he brought it. History ceased to be the subject I loved. My teaching was old hat, according to him. He never said this in so many words but the message was clear. And suddenly everybody seemed to embrace the changes, even the PE teacher who only taught six periods of history a week and was as thick as a plank. I became the outsider and I knew that my number was up. Embrace the new methodology or die. So, what could I do? I had a mortgage the size of the national debt, a new baby, Molly on maternity leave. I couldn't give my job up. I had to find other roles in the school. As it happened, they were looking for a new examinations officer, you know, doing all the paperwork for entering pupils for public exams. Not a full time job but it meant that I taught less. Then I took over the responsibility for timetabling and eventually I gave up my teaching altogether in favour of administrative jobs within the school. They made me a deputy head on the strength of these responsibilities, which meant extra income at a tricky time. Molly was expecting Chris by then. But I think I lost something during those years. I didn't realise how much I would miss teaching. I loved teaching - imparting knowledge, opening up young minds, eliciting insights into the human condition, and those precious times, rare I have to admit, when the topic you were teaching touched something deep within the kids and they fell completely silent and just listened, their eyes on you, rapt in the moment, that awe and wonder moment. It was as if you had turned a key in their minds and unlocked a mystery. And I had given up this experience to become just an administrator. And it wasn't as if my new role was easier. There were still pressures, even if they were different pressures. Deadlines, always deadlines. 'Harry, I need the new timetable asap. Are the exam entries completed? Have you done the health and safety review on school trips.' And there was me with two young children, weighed down with work. And yet Molly thinks I was a good father. I didn't think I was at the time.

CHAPTER 8

Harry was up early because the previous evening, while he and Molly were supposedly watching a period drama that they'd recorded, she was actually pre-occupied with the laptop and he guessed that she was writing him the email that he secretly feared. He tried to glance at what Molly was typing but she'd placed a large cushion to her side to block his view.

'Which one is he?' she asked, pausing to look at the television. 'Is he the heroine's brother or the one she hates at the moment but who's she's bound to marry in the end? They both look the same to me.'

'If you'd concentrate on one task, i.e. watching the drama, instead of doing whatever you're doing on the computer, you'd be able to follow what's going on.'

~

As soon as Molly had left for work, Harry scampered upstairs to the computer. What character assassination awaited him? He scrolled down his emails and, sure enough, there was one from Molly.

Right, following yesterday's paean of praise to your good points, I'm afraid these are (in my opinion) your bad points. Sorry about having to say anything that might hurt you but it's best that I get it all off my chest. I'm starting off with the best of your worst points, if you get my drift. Okay, here goes.

1. You've become very secretive of late. Or maybe 'furtive' is more accurate. If I didn't know you, I'd think you were having an affair? What a ridiculous thought. Or is it? I may have to come back to that one.

2. You are pedantic in the extreme. If I say anything that is even slightly wrong or ambiguous, you correct me. What does it matter if it was Chicken Shack

playing when we met? It might have been the Hallé Orchestra jamming with Billy J Kramer and the Dakotas for all I care. If I say that the weather looks set fair for a stroll in Heath Park this afternoon, I don't need you to say that the weather forecast indicates that an anti-cyclone moving into south Wales will bring light precipitation to the Cardiff area. I've probably said that all wrong and you're mentally correcting me as you read this. And yes, I am exaggerating but that's what women do to get their point across. Do you remember when we went to the Cotswolds for the day with Janice and Doug and we all decided to have an early pub lunch? We found that really old one in Chipping Camden and it was completely empty when we went inside. Doug said: 'It's like the Marie Celeste in here.' And you said: 'Actually, Doug, you're wrong there and it's a common mistake that a lot of people make. It's not Marie Celeste but *Mary* Celeste.' Harry, Doug was only commenting about the pub being empty. He didn't need a history lesson on the correct name of an abandoned ship. Your comment put a damper on the meal and on the whole day. The sad thing is that the only person who didn't notice this was you.

3. You are obsessive and getting worse. Parts of this house are becoming no-go areas for me because you are obsessed with keeping them tidy and in order. I rarely venture into the garage for fear of disturbing something and if I do you follow me in and ask me what I want so that I don't touch anything of yours. It's my garage too, you know. Whenever I load the dishwasher, you wait for me to disappear and then you re-arrange everything, especially the cutlery. Yes, you do! Harry, I haven't got the will to put all the knives, spoons and forks into serried ranks and, yes, I know that it makes it easier to put the cutlery in the drawer but I have a life. You need to get one yourself. And I won't go into your rituals around time. How often do we find ourselves sitting in the car around a corner so that we can arrive at a friend's house at exactly the time agreed? People don't mind if you're not dead on time. When friends

say come at 8.00, they mean 8.00*ish* and that can be up to 15 minutes later before you're being tardy. But you don't do *ish*, do you? You've never done *ish*.

4. I said in the attic that we don't talk any more and you may pedantically say that of course we talk. But you're thinking of the would-you-pass-the-salt kind of talk. That's not what I mean. To me, talking is the oil that lubricates a relationship, that keeps it in working order. You'll probably say that I can talk for both of us but a lot of the time I have to because I can't get anything meaningful from you. Most of the time you just mumble agreement to what I have to say. I didn't marry a 'yes dear' husband. Why can't we have a good argument like we used to? Sometimes, in the past, when we were arguing, I'd know you were right (actually you were right most of the time) but I'd argue the opposite just for the emotional thrill of the whole thing. It made me feel alive. Harry, we used to talk about anything and everything. Now we're like strangers on a train.

5. But all these points are just symptoms of a deeper problem that seems to inhabit you these days. The point I was trying to make in the attic was that you and I met somewhere in another time when we were young. What we felt about each other then changed our lives and determined our future. We married on the strength of it, had kids, signed on for hefty mortgages, got through the various setbacks that life throws at you but eventually reached the higher ground that we all seek. Touch wood, we could have another 25 years together (okay, not the most persuasive argument at the present) but we should be enjoying each other's company and we're clearly not. I think I could put up with your being pedantic, obsessive and unresponsive if I thought that it gave you any pleasure in life. But I don't think it does. I think that you are very unhappy and that hurts me more than your faults irritate me. I want back the man who used to be my husband, my helpmate and, above all, my friend. And, though there are times when I could scream at you, more often than not I

want to weep for you. Something needs to change, Harry, something needs to change.

Love,

Molly

Harry continued to stare at the screen long after he'd finished reading the message.

~

The evening meal was eaten in silence, Molly's email occupying the empty chair next to Harry like Banquo's ghost. Harry was waiting for the right moment to talk about going over to France. He knew that Molly did not relish Brittany at this time of year, closing up the cottage for the winter being a chore that she hated. However, Harry took pleasure in the cottage's seclusion, the lack of a phone signal, the absence of neighbours and friends, the long, dark evenings around the fire. He always wanted to stay longer but he sensed that, with the tension existing between Molly and himself, he would need to compromise on this occasion. He cleared his throat but it was Molly who spoke.

'Harry, I've decided not to go to the cottage with you.'

Dear Leonard,

I was talking about my shortcomings as a father, wasn't I? When you have a child you have all sorts of expectations about the parent you will be but being a good parent is not guaranteed however much effort you put into it. Maybe my generation tended to over think everything. I sometimes wonder about my own father, whether he gave much thought to the task of parenting. Probably none. But whether you read the manual or just wing it, you still leave a legacy. My father was a lorry driver. He had driven trucks in the war and it was natural that he should look for a driving job when he was demobbed. He used to do a lot of trips into south Wales. It was a long journey from Torrington because there was no bridge over the river Severn in those days. You had to go all around Gloucester to get into Wales. There were no motorways in that area either and few bypasses, so I think he spent a lot of time getting stuck in slow-moving traffic in towns and villages. I think that's why, when the schools were on holiday, he would ask me to go with him, for company you see. He was proud of being a lorry driver, with all the knowledge he had acquired about the highways and byways of the south west, and he probably wanted to impress me and encourage me to take up the same job when I left school. But I hated going with him and made every excuse possible to get out of it. But sometimes I had to go with him. My mother would give me one of her looks, which said you're going with your Dad whether you like it or not.

But I still hated it. We would set off in the dark and when I climbed into the cab of his Foden flatbed lorry with an Oxo tin full of sandwiches and a flask of tea, I would almost retch with the smell of diesel and cigarette smoke. My father smoked roll-ups and he always had a wet cigarette sticking to his lip as we drove through the winding roads of the west country. Although my father may have wanted me with him, he rarely spoke to me on these journeys. I was like one of those soft toys that drivers sometimes hang in the windows of their cabs. Having shunned breakfast to get onto the road as quickly as possible, his first stop was the nearest transport café. It was a meeting place for all the drivers heading out that day. The smell of fat and smoke hit you as you walked in and all the other drivers would have to comment on my being there. 'Got your apprentice today, have you, Jack?' 'Bout time you fed him up, Jack. He's like a matchstick with the wood scraped off.' We would sit at a grubby formica table, its surface all chipped and ringed with tea stains and Dad would order the greasiest breakfast on offer, while I would usually have a couple of pieces of toast, just to stop him nagging me to eat something. He wouldn't just let me sit there while he ate. The other drivers would try to outdo each other with dirty jokes, the punch lines of which I didn't for the life of me understand, but they liked embarrassing 'Jack's lad'.

Back in the cab my father would tell me to pay them no mind but I knew he was embarrassed, too. He wanted me to grow into a strapping lad who could eat a hearty breakfast, arm wrestle all his mates and sink ten pints in the Black Horse every night. He told me he would talk to his boss when the time was right and get me a start on the lorries. But, of course, I was a weedy boy who couldn't arm wrestle a fly and I was more interested in books than joining my Dad in the smelly cab of his truck. Things got worse when I passed the 11-plus exam and went to Bideford Grammar School. My mother was proud as punch but I could see the distance that already existed between my father and me widen into a great chasm that would never be bridged.

My father's credo was to never forget your roots, never to get above yourself. The grammar school strived to do the opposite and my father could never come to terms with this. He would scornfully pick up my French textbook, flip the pages and pronounce on the uselessness of teaching a foreign language to a Torrington boy. I think there was a scarcely concealed jealously in him, too, that I was acquiring more knowledge week by week than he had gained in a lifetime and he thought it made him a smaller man in everyone's eyes. I once heard my mother tell him to go easy on me, to stop deriding my studies. 'You'll lose him, Jack, if you're not careful.' My father replied: 'The boy's lost already.'

My father never saw me grow into a young man, never saw the chasm between us bridged, which it might have been. In the big freeze of 1963, having returned late at night from an arduous journey to Port Talbot steelworks over frozen roads, he took out his lorry early the following day. Like a lot of his mates, he had been laid off during that severe winter with blocked roads and treacherous conditions. So he jumped at the chance of another load. At the last minute he asked me to go with him, something he hadn't done for years. It was only a short journey. We'd be back by early afternoon. I nearly said yes, because I saw that this was a sort of peace offering, an acceptance of what I was but still a gesture from father to son. But I said no and gave him the lame excuse of having a lot of homework to get in by Monday. I told him I couldn't afford the time. I remember that look of disappointment etched on his face. 'All right, son. Maybe when the weather breaks, eh?'

My father's lorry jack-knifed on the A361, just outside Tiverton. At the inquest the view was that my father probably fell asleep at the wheel and a verdict of accidental death was recorded. In his summing-up, the Coroner concluded, as if this was any consolation, that he probably died instantly.

CHAPTER 9

The N12 from Morlaix to Guingamp was unusually busy that morning but Harry was oblivious to the traffic as he ambled along in the inside lane. He was deep in thought. The overnight crossing from Plymouth to Roscoff had been rough and he had rolled around on his bunk all night, his stomach protesting at the one too many nightcaps of Armagnac that he had swallowed in the bar before retiring. He'd foolishly pulled down the top bunk, as was his wont, before remembering that Molly wasn't with him this time and he could sleep below. In his drunken state he couldn't get the top bunk back into the ceiling and was rewarded with a bang on the head when he went to the toilet in the night.

In spite of a queasy stomach Harry still had the complimentary breakfast on the boat. It was a habit and there was the fact that he was getting something gratis from the ferry company, which he did not hold in high regard. Harry did not think he had much in common with the hundreds of French property owners who, like he and Molly, regularly crossed from Plymouth to Roscoff. But get together with them in the bar on an overnight crossing and before you'd left Plymouth Sound they were all complaining about the ferry company. 'Bloody ferry. These prices are getting ridiculous.' It was always the same story, so the complimentary breakfast for property owners was a must have.

Harry's stomach had told him that a full English (especially the French version) would be a risky venture. Normally he looked forward to collecting on his tray a breakfast whose component parts – bacon, eggs, sausage, hash browns, juice, tea, toast and butter –

equalled to the last cent the sum that the ferry company so generously allowed. Molly, however, did not play the same game and, between mouthfuls, Harry would point out the errors of her under- or over-spending.

'If you'd had a roll instead of all that toast you wouldn't have had to pay anything. You're not going to waste that butter, are you?'

'Harry, you know I don't usually eat a big breakfast, especially one full of fat, but if I don't spend the allowance you moan at me and you moan at me if I have to pay anything extra. I'm not going to walk around with a calculator on my tray at six o'clock in the morning just to satisfy your obsessive nature.'

'It's seven o'clock.'

'What?'

'It's seven o'clock. We're on French time now. You haven't put your watch forward.'

As Harry motored along the N12, his mind was cast back to last weekend when Molly had broken the news that she would not be coming to France with him. They had owned the cottage for over ten years. It was bought with their joint retirements in mind. They always went together.

'The thing is, Harry, I need some time on my own. I've got things to sort out in my mind, you know, the *things* I keep trying to talk to you about. We were only going over for five days, just to tackle a few jobs and shut the place up for the winter. I only get in your way at the best of times, doing things in the wrong order, not following your spreadsheet. If you remember last year I dared to do Task 4b when Task 4a had not been properly completed and ticked off.'

'That's true but we always go over to France together and the crossing's booked with you as a passenger…'

'Harry, the ferry company's been paid whether I go or not. And anyway that side of it is not important. The important thing is that I want to be on my own for a few days and make some decisions, about me, about us and about our future.'

'Our future? What about our future?' This was unknown territory for Harry. 'What are you planning to do?' he asked.

'I don't know. It could be something or everything. I might decide to continue as I am, although that's unlikely under the present circumstances. I might go off with a 30-year-old gigolo, go trekking along the Inca Trail to Machu Pichu or join a lesbian commune, and live in a tepee in mid-Wales…'

'But you're not a lesbian.'

'I know but I could help them out when they're busy.' Molly laughed out loud at this remark, which she thought quite clever. This unnerved Harry even more and Molly was a little saddened to see the perplexed look on his face.

'Look, Harry, the bottom line is that something has to change between us and at the moment I don't sense that the change is going to come from your side. So, I've got to do that something before I explode. And you wouldn't want to find bits of me covering the walls and ceiling when you come home one day, would you?'

And there it had been left. Molly was adamant about the whole thing and there was nothing that Harry could do about it. The cottage could not be ignored and so he would have to go alone.

Molly was not fond of the ferry crossing, even when she could sleep her way through the six-hour journey. Being woken up in their cramped cabin by the ferry's muzak at an ungodly hour didn't help matters and, in spite of Harry speeding her along with the urgency of a drill sergeant, they usually had to endure a long wait to disembark because fate always seemed to place their vehicle on the car deck that disgorged its passengers last. She would huddle her coat around her, with Harry cursing impatiently beside her, as they waited for the crew members to release them from their purgatory. At this time of year it was still pitch dark and by the time they were skirting Morlaix to join the N12, sleep would inevitably overcome her, however much she tried to keep awake. Harry could do the hour-long drive to the cottage blindfold, so he needed no navigator but he felt that she should have the courtesy to stay awake. Molly knew that her dozing off irritated him but once her eyelids grew heavy she was gone.

Harry glanced at the empty passenger seat and wouldn't have minded if Molly was comatose, so long as she was sitting there. He thought back to when he had met her. He was in his first year at Cardiff and was still emerging from the chrysalis that turned a shy, bookish sixth-former into a full-blown, late 1960s student. The process began with a change of nomenclature. Overnight, Henry had become Harry. He was growing his hair but it looked like he was wearing it for a friend. His clothes were still distinctly casual rather than trendy, his jeans worn with black shoes rather than desert boots. But he was getting there. He had the beginnings of a wispy beard and had swapped his briefcase for a canvas shoulder bag, even though a number of his fellow students had felt the weight of its swinging bulk as he hurried clumsily along the corridors of the history department late for a lecture.

The biggest change that Harry experienced was in music. He had thought himself well prepared for college life, steeped as he was in the Beatles, the Stones and the Who but his hall of residence echoed to the more esoteric strains of progressive blues: John Mayall and Cream and, of course, the demigod who outshone the whole pantheon: Eric Clapton. Harry took some time to adjust but he was desperate to be an acolyte of this new musical order and so he nodded approvingly when he was introduced to the strains of Disraeli Gears in someone's room late at night.

A friend told him that Chicken Shack were playing at the students' union and it was clear that they were a band on the approved list so he agreed to go. It was a mid-week concert and the audience was thin but Chicken Shack seemed blasé about the attendance. Stan Webb apologised for the late start, the aftermath of a rather liquid lunch he said. Everyone laughed at that and waited patiently for the band to set up. Harry was taken by the girl at the piano and someone whispered: 'That's Christine Perfect.' Harry nodded approvingly. The only live music that Harry had ever witnessed was at school events when a local band or, worse, a school 'beat' group as the teachers called it, would try their hand at the pop hits of the day. But Chicken Shack were different.

The band eventually got underway and Stan Webb began to weave his magic, moving in and out of the rapt audience by means of an extra long guitar lead. This is different, thought Harry. For the first time he began to really distinguish a band's component parts: Webb's slowhand guitar solos, the undercurrent of bass and drum, the rolling piano that played fast and loose with guitar and harmonica… and then Christine Perfect's smoky vocals pierced the even smokier atmosphere:

I guess you really don't want me, I'm just an unlucky so-and-so.

Harry was smitten. He loved the blues, he loved Stan Webb and he adored Christine Perfect.

Chicken Shack played a couple of encores and then told the audience to go home. They had to be in Newcastle the following day. The lights went up but Harry lingered. He wanted to hold on to the moment. A few seats away sat a girl who was vaguely familiar – maybe he'd seen her in the humanities department. She was petite, with long dark hair and, like Harry, seemed caught in the moment while her two friends were gathering up their things. Girls frightened Harry but this girl was different and, after all, he and she were sharing some mutually aesthetic experience. For Harry this was a road to Damascus moment. The girl might have been wishing she'd stayed home to finish that essay but Harry knew otherwise. He would speak with her, talk about the band and ask her to have a drink with him. He rose from his seat and moved towards her but sadly his courage failed him and he walked past shyly, only to have to double back because he's left his scarf on the seat. But he thought she glanced at him with half a smile as he passed her for the second time.

In the students' union next day, Harry was amazed to see the girl again, engrossed in a book, which he took to be foreign because he could just see the word 'Tolkien' on the cover. He had to say something – this was too coincidental.

'Did you enjoy the concert last night?' Why did he say 'concert'? How uncool. 'You know, Chicken Shack.'

The girl could have given him a polite put-down, ignored him completely or screamed for help, but to Harry's surprise, she did none of these.

'Yes, they were great, weren't they? Do you know their music well? I'm new to them, I'm afraid.'

'I've heard some of their stuff,' Harry lied 'but after last night I think I'll get their album. What did you think of Stan Webb?'

Harry had already surpassed the number of words he had ever spoken to all the girls of his acquaintance and this particular girl was still listening to him. He sat down next to her and she didn't recoil in horror. Her name was Molly, she was a second-year English student, she came from Hereford and, sorry, she had a lecture in five minutes. This is it, thought Harry, as she stood up to go. But, as she picked up her books, she said:

'The Moody Blues are at the Top Rank on Saturday. I was going to go but my friends hate them.'

Harry paused for what seemed an age. Molly was looking at him intently, with a fixed half-smile. He could feel his cheeks flushing. Finally he blurted:

'…um, I fancied seeing them, too. I could take…I mean we could go together if you've got no one to go with.'

'Great. I'll meet you outside Boot's at half past seven.'

And that's how it started.

I bet she won't turn up, Harry thought, as he waited for a gap in the traffic moving slowly along Queen Street. But there she was, waiting quietly and not even glancing in all directions, as Harry would have done. She was expecting him to come. It was one of the first things that Harry noticed about Molly – the economy of her being herself. Some would say she was quiet and reserved but she had an inner confidence. She took up a small space and she expended little effort in being the person she was. Her movements were measured, her talk sufficient and her laughter infectious but contained.

The Moody Blues were supported by the Bedrocks who had had a minor hit by covering the Beatles' Ob La Di Ob La Di. This was as incongruous a bill as Russ Conway supporting The Who and most of the crowd showed their disdain for a reggae band by adjourning to the bar. When the Moody Blues finally came on, the atmosphere changed because they were on the approved list. Harry saw little of the group because he spent most of their set looking at Molly's face. Having been in the girl's company for at least three hours, he felt qualified to pass judgement on her womanhood. Molly was not classically pretty but her face had a serenity that made him catch his breath. Emboldened by the wistful melodies of the Moody Blues and three pints of Tartan bitter, Harry leaned across and gently kissed Molly's cheek. Keeping her gaze firmly fixed on Justin Hayward's face, framed by his blond halo, Molly whispered: 'Thank you, Harry' and squeezed his hand. Christine Perfect had been relegated to second place.

Harry and Molly shared a bag of chips on the walk home. Molly lived in a house off Senghenydd Road with three other girls. Harry thought how grown-up it was to have your own place. His hall of residence seemed juvenile by comparison. She opened a bottle of Hirondelle and Harry pronounced its cloying sweetness very palatable. They sat on the single bed and he kissed her again.

Harry could remember everything that happened. Molly allowed him some ineffectual fumblings before calling a halt: 'Let's get to know each other better first, shall we?' She rose, adjusted her clothes and put an LP on the record player. It was the first time that Harry had come across this particular artist. The songs were like nothing he had ever heard, the lyrics poetic, the music somnolent but strangely compelling. But it was the

80

voice that sent a thrill through him, if you could call it a voice. It penetrated deep into his being, flowing through his consciousness with a sensation that both soothed and stirred him.

Harry was in no hurry as he made his way back to his hall of residence. He and Molly had arranged to meet at the Scott Memorial in Roath Park the following day for a Sunday afternoon stroll around the lake. As he headed up towards Penylan Hill, he walked into a fine drizzle that was blowing across the Bristol Channel and over the packed terraces of Splott, Adamsdown and Roath, bringing with it the tang of smoke and ash that it had picked up as it wound its way through East Moors steelworks. Harry walked along with measured steps, his hands deep in the pockets of his army surplus greatcoat, and did not break the rhythm of his stride as the incline grew steeper. He reached the top of Penylan Hill and before turning into his hall of residence he paused. He looked across the city below him, picking out the landmarks he already recognised, like the dome of City Hall and the grey starkness of the Pearl Assurance tower, and determined to become more familiar with this place. He was at the beginning of a relationship that he knew would sustain and support him for the rest of his life. He had met someone who finally understood him, someone who could steer him through the choppy waters of life. And with Molly at his side as well, surely nothing could go wrong.

It must be said that at the time the significance of the moment escaped Harry but the memory of it embedded itself in his mind like a limpet on a sea-washed rock.

Dear Leonard,

My mother was devastated by my father's death. I don't think she ever got over it. Her one consolation, she said, was that I could have died in the accident, too. That was no consolation to me. Life became harder for us. There was no real money coming in any more. We got a small amount of cash from an insurance policy that my mother used to pay into every week, to a man who called to the door. And some of my father's mates had a whip-round for us but the money didn't last for long. I came downstairs from my room one night and I could hear my mother talking in the sitting room to her sister, my aunt Louie. The subject was money and how difficult things were – that was becoming a very popular topic of conversation since my father's death. My mother was saying that we just couldn't manage. We lived in a council house and the rent had just gone up. She was at her wits' end, she said. My aunt was trying to comfort her by saying that there were only two years to go before I left school. I was thirteen at the time and it had never occurred to me that I would leave school at fifteen. In my head I had three years before my 'O' levels and then another two for 'A' levels. I already knew that I wanted to be a teacher.

My aunt was older than my mother and had two strapping sons, John and James, who were in their twenties. Whenever I saw them, which was rare if I had my way, they always tried to take a rise out of me. 'Hello, Henry, have your balls dropped yet?' And they would grab me between the legs. 'What's that you've got there, Henry, a chipolata?' I hated them. On one visit, one of them must have sneaked into my bedroom because when I opened my French textbook, there was crude cock and balls drawn all over the front page.

Anyway, they both worked in a big creamery nearby and what my aunt Louie was saying was that they could get me a start as soon as I left school. That would bring in some much-needed money. I was mortified. I had visions of what my two cousins would do to me on a daily basis. I had heard tales of what happened to young kids when they started work in factories. It was a sort of initiation ceremony. Sometimes they would pull your trousers down and cover your balls with grease. But I knew John and James would do far worse. They hated their grammar school snob of a cousin and I would probably end up drowned in a vat of cream.

'What's Henry doing in the cream, John?'

'The breast stroke, I think, James.'

But, as I listened, I could see that my leaving school at fifteen was the only solution. How could I see my mother working her fingers to the bone and me, like some Little Lord Fauntleroy, continuing my studies in the grammar school and then university, with no prospect of bringing any money home for the next ten years? It just wouldn't work.

But then my mother piped up and told aunt Louie in no uncertain terms that she was not going to take me out of the grammar school. That was not what she wanted and my father would turn in his grave if that happened. She didn't know how she would do it but Henry would stay in school if she had to scrub floors for the rest of her life. Aunt Louie said that my mother was stupid and that she had always tried to be better than anyone else in the family. She had ideas above her station.

I never felt more proud of my mother than that day, listening outside the door. And so I carried on at the grammar school and I worked hard. I won prizes at Speech Days for History and English and, sitting apart

83

from the parents with the other prize-winners, I would look round for my mother. She would walk into the school hall nervously, with her best coat on, her hair having been set by the lady down the road, a woman completely at odds with her surroundings, the panelled walls with their huge honours boards commemorating the old boys who had been killed in the two world wars, the boys who had won scholarships to Oxford and Cambridge, the masters in their hoods and gowns, the civic dignitaries full of their own importance sitting on the stage. When my name was called for whatever prize I'd won, I could feel her eyes upon me as I walked from my seat, up the steps to the stage, where I would shake the guest speaker's hand, take the prize proffered to me and walk across the stage and back to my seat. Afterwards, I would hurry to the school canteen where parents were mingling with cups of tea and biscuits, knowing that my mother would be desperately uncomfortable and straining to see me come to her rescue.

She would never hug or kiss me as parents do so readily today. We just didn't do that kind of thing in those days. She would look at the prize I had won, usually a dry and dusty history book, and opening it at the frontispiece where a calligraphic inscription would attest to my prowess in the subject, she would just smile and say, 'Your father would be very proud.' And I would feel such pangs of pain in the pit of my stomach, for my father who could never tell me what he felt about me and for my mother who was prepared to do anything to keep me on the path that would only take me ever further from her.

CHAPTER 10

Brélidy, the village in which Harry and Molly had their cottage, was just off the D8 about ten minutes' drive north of Guingamp. Harry loved to tell people that Guingamp gives us the word 'gingham' because the town was famous for the red and white checked cloth that was woven there in the middle ages. As a former history teacher, he didn't quite believe this himself but if anyone disputed the fact he would tell them to type 'Guingamp' in a word document and see what the spellchecker suggested. 'Gingham', he would say. 'It offers you gingham.'

To describe the village of Brélidy as nondescript would be unkind but if you did the three hundred or so inhabitants would probably not light torches and come for you after dark. The last excitement they experienced was in 1347 when King Edward IV invaded Brittany in the middle of the Hundred Years' War and that didn't actually affect Brélidy because the main action was the siege of La Roche Derrien, which was just up the road. The coming of the railway might have been the next significant event but even then the village had to share its station with its nearest neighbour, the village of Plouëc du Trieux. And even though the station is called Brélidy-Plouëc, it's in Plouëc, not Brélidy.

These considerations did not affect Harry and Molly when they decided to buy 'Pont Camarel', a tiny cottage at the bottom of the lane that leads to a shrine dedicated to an Irish saint who brought Christianity to Brittany in the sixth century. Molly loved the cottage's quaintness; Harry its seclusion. The cottage was close to the village but not part of it. For Molly 'Pont Camarel' promised chocolate-box perfection outside but all mod cons inside. For Harry it was all about peace, tranquillity and more peace and tranquillity.

In actual fact, the cottage was not strictly secluded. If you walked further up the lane and crossed the bridge that gave the cottage its name, you came upon another house occupied by a French couple. 'Harry, how wonderful,' said Molly, when they first looked at their house. 'We've got French neighbours. We can practise our French with them. I'm sure they're going to be very friendly.' This wasn't a cert because, even in Brittany, there was sometimes a groundswell of Gallic shrugs as more and more Brits moved in to take over run-down properties, snapped up at bargain prices. 'You'll never guess. Picked up a house in France – needs renovating, but it's got three acres, a grenier, a cider press and out buildings – and all for twenty thou.'

Harry and Molly's neighbours did not harbour any bad feelings towards the new occupants of 'Pont Camarel.' Guillaume and Sylvie were only too pleased to see the cottage being lived in. They did not want to see the place go to rack and ruin. Molly and Sylvie immediately hit it off. It was less so with Harry and Guillaume. To Guillaume, Britain was a country still infested with mad cow disease, a baleful health service and a railway network that only worked properly when a French company took parts of it over. Guillaume was not backward in airing these views when thc two couples got together for aperitifs, a strictly observed custom at either home which started promptly at 6.30pm and had to be over within the hour. Harry hated it because Guillaume and Sylvie's English was far better than his French and he disliked Guillaume's Britain bashing. Molly would tell Harry not to take the bait but he was always glad when the allotted time was over. As they walked back to the cottage over the

86

bridge Harry would invariably say: 'What happened in 1940, eh? Glad of our help then, weren't they?'

As he turned off the N12 onto the Tréguier road, Harry mused about Molly and women of her age. They were a mystery, of course. That was common knowledge. He had worked with female teachers all his life and they could be a nightmare. He remembered the problem he had had with kettles in classrooms. In his role as Health and Safety Officer, he could not ignore the fact that some teachers, mainly the older female ones he observed, kept a kettle in their classroom to make the cups of tea that fuelled them through the day. The practice had gone on for years without comment but Harry's latest H&S bulletin spelled out the dangers when boiling water and children are in close proximity. Harry informed the Head of the need to ban the kettles. The Head accepted there was an H&S issue here but would have preferred to tell the staff that they could retain their kettles as long as they kept them in a cupboard. But Harry stuck to his guns and the Head reluctantly agreed that he should memo everyone. The memo was one of his best, he thought, the arguments meticulously laid out, the dangers graphically illustrated, the conclusion irrefutable. However, the furore engendered amongst the women staff took Harry by surprise. There were visitations to his office, remarkable in itself since few teachers knew where Harry's office was. They couldn't possibly give up their kettles for a myriad of reasons, the foremost being the scrum in the staff room at break times, which prevented them from making a much-needed cup of tea if they were on duty. The staff room was too far from their teaching room anyway and during a free period they preferred to take a cuppa in their classroom while they did their marking. Harry looked at their bobbing faces and the blur of their dangling earrings as they described the affront his memo had caused. They were, after all, *professionals*, and how dare he suggest that they would ever put the safety of a *child* in their care at risk. Harry knew that once a teacher spoke the hallowed word *child* in a breathy whisper he was on shaky ground. That evening he told Molly about his day and how unreasonable the female staff had been. But far from agreeing with him, she took their side and even suggested that his approach had been wrong. Perhaps the issue would have been best raised in a staff meeting where everyone could have discussed it and Harry's arguments might still have been carried. An email in a workplace can often be misinterpreted.

Then there were Molly's female friends and he had to admit that, in spite of Molly's recent strange behaviour, she was probably the most normal out of all of them. Jean, for example, had led a life devoid of incident, being the dutiful wife and mother par excellence. Then, without warning, she had run off with one of Harry's best friends, decamped to Spain and was now running a bar on the Costa Dorada. Harry could not understand it because Jean's husband, Bob, was the nicest bloke you could meet, a doyen of the pub quiz league and an avid collector of vintage postcards.

As Harry turned down the lane from the village, he felt the usual twinge of anxiety when the cottage had been unoccupied for any length of time. Would everything be all right? What if there had been a burglary and Guillaume and Sylvie had not noticed? Or a leak? Or a fallen tree? Harry and Molly rented out the cottage each summer but the last visitors had gone nearly five weeks ago. They had a caretaker of sorts, a Brit who lived nearby but he had gone down south for the winter. The lane was covered in a carpet of bronze leaves that made it look like an ancient trackway and if a hooded pilgrim with a staff had loomed into view Harry wouldn't have been surprised. As Harry came upon the shrine, the cottage came into view. The shutters gave it a forlorn air but in the low autumn sunlight that broke through the cloud at that moment it still touched Harry with its quaint rusticity, as it had done when he and Molly first saw it.

Harry's first job was to remove the shutters, which released great shafts of light into the interior, catching the motes of dust that Harry's movements had disturbed. Next he fired up the log burner with dry wood that he had brought with him, experience having taught him that his woodpile might be damp. The burner quickly crackled into life as the air rushed through the damper. Lighting a fire always gave him a primeval thrill. It was what made the cottage come alive. Evenings could not be spent without one and it gave him a sense of purpose, keeping the fire burning, controlling the flames, regulating the log burner's heat, ensuring the supply of dry wood was constant.

'You give that fire more attention than me,' Molly would say half in jest, as she looked up from her book or took a sip of wine.

Harry was surprised by how his thoughts kept turning to Molly and he had barely arrived. Best to keep busy, he thought. He threw open the windows and set to cleaning the tiled floor, even through the last guests had left the place immaculate, but he needed to keep occupied. After only an hour's brushing and mopping, with the car emptied and the bed made up, he had done all he needed to do to make the house habitable once more. He glanced through the side window that overlooked the lane as it curved its way towards the bridge that separated his property from Guillaume's and was suddenly spooked as he saw Guillaume himself striding towards the house. He must have spotted the car, thought Harry. Normally, a visit from his neighbour would not have fazed him unduly but he knew that Molly's absence would be queried and he hadn't thought of what he would say.

Harry dashed out to head off his neighbour before he could enter the house. Guillaume must have thought Harry was unusually friendly as he pumped his neighbour's hand and they exchanged their greetings.

'I see the car. Are you staying long? Sylvie was saying this morning that she had not see Molly for long time.'

Right, here goes, thought Harry.

'Molly is not with me. Her father is not well and she had to stay in Cardiff to look after him. She was disappointed not to come but we were only coming over for a few days anyway.'

Guillaume gave him a long, lingering look. He doesn't believe me, thought Harry, as a bead of sweat trickled down his back.

'C'est dommage,' Guillaume said eventually, turning to go. 'Sylvie is making the shopping. Come over this evening for a drink.'

Harry spent the rest of the day replenishing his woodpile with chopped wood, mowing the front lawn and doing a bit of hacking back around the cottage. The mild, damp Breton climate was perfect for growth. Leave the cottage for six months and you'll never find it again, Harry would say to Molly, so vigorous were the laurel bushes outside the house and the brambles at the back were always threatening to block out the windows with their triffid-like growth. Harry sprayed the brambles on every visit but he only succeeded in limiting their growth. Even napalm would struggle to do the job.

Harry made his aperitif visit as short as possible that evening. Sylvie kept asking after Molly and her father. The falsehood about his illness made Harry uncomfortable because he didn't want to tempt fate with someone who for his age was in hearty good health. But Sylvie wanted to know the ins and outs of his condition. What was the prognosis? Was he in hospital? What treatment was being prescribed? Would he be all right considering his age? Harry baulked at having his father-in-law being admitted to hospital but needed an illness that was convincing enough to cause concern.

'It started with a fall in the sheltered accommodation. His eyesight is not good these days. He was not badly hurt, a few bruises and a sprained wrist, but the shock seemed to bring on influenza and Molly was worried that it might turn to pneumonia, so she felt she had to stay at home. The doctor also thought that she should cancel the trip, just in case.'

Harry was pleased with his response but he had voiced it without taking a breath and with so much gesturing that he might have been in a Victorian melodrama. It did not satisfy Sylvie one bit and Guillaume shot her a glance that said I told you he was acting strangely.

Harry was relieved to make his exit, saying that he had some supper cooking in the oven. In truth, he had nothing prepared and he wasn't that hungry anyway. Returning to the cottage, he found that the wood burner had gone out and the chill November air seemed to have percolated through every pore of the house. Instead of relighting the fire, he poured himself the stiffest of whiskies and took it and the bottle to bed. As he struggled to warm up under the quilt, he was reminded of what Joni had to say when the one you love is not with you:

The bed's too big, the frying pan's too wide.

Dear Leonard,

I remember that it was in my final year at university that I began to notice changes in my mother. She seemed to be tired all the time, which was strange because when I was younger she always had loads of energy. But she made little of it and I just put it down to her growing old.

I was wrapped up with Molly all the time then. We were planning to move into a flat together in Cardiff. She was finishing her year's teacher training and I already had a place in the education department to do mine once I'd finished my degree. My mother hadn't met Molly, although every time I went home she would ask when she could meet my 'young lady'. It was just after my final exams when Molly said it was time that she met my mother, as we were moving ahead in our relationship. I had already met her parents. I was scared to death that any mention of living together would get me tarred and feathered but they were very easy about it. Times were changing, they said, and as long as we were ready for this step, they were fine.

It was going to be more difficult with my mother. She had been brought up very strictly and was having nothing to do with the mores of the swinging sixties. When I told her that Molly and I were coming to stay, she said that Molly could have my sister Susan's old room. The previous year she had married a lance corporal in the Royal Engineers and they were now stationed in Osnabrück, Germany. Molly told me she didn't mind about the sleeping arrangements; it was my mother's house, after all.

I hadn't seen my mother for a few months. I'd stayed in Cardiff for the Easter vacation because I'd found some part-time work in a bar to earn some cash for our impending moving in together. We caught the bus from the railway station and Molly could see how nervous I was. I'd never brought a girl home before. My anxiety was not to do with what my mother thought of Molly. That was never going to be a problem. I realised that I was afraid of my mother embarrassing me, of trying too hard to be something that she wasn't. We arrived to find the dining table laid for tea – a white damask cloth, the best china and the table groaning with food. It would have fed an army on manoeuvres. My mother kept telling Molly to eat up, she needed to put more meat on her bones. Molly took it all in her stride and, when my mother left the room to re-fill the teapot, she told me to calm down. Everything was fine. Of course, Molly and my mother hit it off straightaway as I suppose I knew they would.

When we had cleared up and were in the sitting room with another of the endless cups of tea that my mother loved to make, Molly surprised me by launching into the issue of moving in together. She said men were pretty hopeless at these kinds of things, so she'd make the first move.

'Henry and I…'(that was the best start she could make because to my mother I was always Henry) …would like to get married some day…' (that was news to me because we'd never discussed it) … 'but we would like some time to get to know each other, to really know whether we are suited to each other. So we plan to live together first and, in the absence of Henry's father, we would really love to have your blessing for what we intend to do.'

My mother was putty in Molly's hands. She wept, she said she couldn't think of a nicer girl for me and we could have her blessing a million fold. That evening we sat and watched a bit of television but by nine o'clock my mother said she'd turn in as she'd had a busy day. I didn't think much of it but once my mother had gone upstairs Molly took my hand and said that my mother wasn't well. I mumbled something about it being nothing to worry about, she was just a bit tired, but Molly squeezed my hand tighter and made me look her in the face. She said:

'Harry, I'm not talking about tiredness. Your mother is ill and she needs treatment urgently.'

I never found out how Molly knew this and she never told me. I think something unspoken passed between my mother and her that day. The next day Molly and my mother went to the local doctor and by the evening they had a bed for her in the hospital. But it was too late. The specialist told us that my mother's breast and stomach cancer was in an advanced state. He said frankly, with the agony she was in, he didn't know how she had endured the last few weeks. She would have been aware that something was radically wrong with her a long time ago, maybe even 18 months before. Why she had done nothing about it was impossible to say. But the only thing that could be done now was to make her comfortable because it would not be long.

Molly and I were sitting in silence in a waiting room at the hospital having a cup of tepid tea while the nurses were seeing to my mother.

'It's you.' she finally said.

'What?'

'Your mother did nothing about her illness and just kept going because of you. This is your final year. She knew how important it was that nothing disturbed your studies. So she's been hanging on, taking each day at a time, until she could hang on no longer but she got there. You've just finished your exams and so she could finally give in to it. She must have had extraordinary courage and determination to do that. It was her last duty as a mother to see you through university and to see you settled.'

'Settled?'

'With me, you ninny. With me.'

My mother died five days after meeting Molly.

CHAPTER 11

In the morning, Harry felt a little better and convinced himself that yesterday's feelings of gloom were partly the result of the bumpy crossing and inadequate sleep. Today looked better already. With a cup of tea in bed and the curtain drawn back, he could see the morning sun breaking through the trees across the lane, illuminating their russet and gold foliage and causing the raindrops that casually fell from their branches to sparkle. Today would be different. He would not risk the gloom descending on him again by staying around the house. He would take himself out and about, perhaps to the sea and maybe to look at chain saws in the DIY shops.

Harry drove into Guingamp and picked up essentials at Lidl before moving to LeClerc across the road where he could kill some more time. It was a blustery day, the eddying wind sending shoppers scurrying to their cars, heads down, as they struggled to steer their laden trolleys. Harry was glad to get inside the warmth of the store. He wandered aimlessly around the aisles, paying no particular attention to anything and feeling less positive about the day. In the end, he decided that the only way to lift his mood was to return to the cottage and absorb himself with all the tasks he'd been putting off. He was just about the close the tailgate of his car when he heard a voice behind him.

'Excuse me, are you British? I noticed the plates of your car. I was hoping you could help me.'

Harry turned round to find a woman, fiftyish he thought, swathed in scarves against the cold, a suitcase at her side, looking at him in a somewhat anguished manner, her eyes pinched in the wind.

'The thing is, I was on my way to Roscoff to catch the ferry. But, damned nuisance, my car broke down on the N12.' She indicated the road with a sweep of her arm but Harry knew quite well that the N12 ran just behind LeClerc and in fact its traffic could be heard thundering along its length as she spoke. 'They've towed my car to a garage and think they'll be able to fix it today but I'm looking for a hotel for the night. Do you know where the nearest one might be or at least where I can find the tourist information office?'

'What was the problem, with the car I mean?'

'No good asking me, I'm afraid. There was a clunk, a red light came on and I just ground to a halt. I need to find somewhere and get out of this cold. I was standing on the N12 for hours and I'm frozen to the marrow.'

As she finished speaking she pulled her woollen hat further down over her ears and turned up the collar of her coat against the wind.

Harry pondered the woman's original question. He was not familiar with Guingamp's hotels but he knew that the tourist office was on the other side of the town, near the Hotel de Ville, because he always passed it on his way out of town and back to the cottage. It wouldn't be a problem to drop her off, would it?

But seated in the car for the short journey across town, the woman seemed to have imposed on Harry a sense of duty to see her settled somewhere and this feeling was magnified when she asked if he wouldn't mind waiting while she enquired in the tourist office. He quickly realised that, without her car, she would need a lift to whichever pension or hotel was suitable and he would have to oblige. But it was common decency, after all. It had now come on to rain heavily and, as she flopped back into the passenger seat clutching a scribbled map of Guingamp and its environs, she looked in an even sorrier state.

'There's not much to choose from, I'm afraid,' she said wearily. 'A lot of the hotels are shut for the winter and what's left look rather seedy. But thank you anyway. It was very kind of you to give me a lift. I'll get my case and leave you in peace. The first on the list is only about a half a mile away apparently.'

Harry's mind was racing. He asked himself what Molly would do in this situation. This woman was well spoken, smartly dressed (at least she looked smart to him) and respectable. Yes, that was the word – respectable. Molly would not hesitate to take her back to the cottage, give her a bowl of soup and let her have one of the rooms upstairs for the night. It was only for one night, after all. As she got out of the car to retrieve her case from the boot, Harry got out, too.

'Wait a moment,' he said. 'I just don't like the idea of you traipsing around this town looking for somewhere to stay, and in this weather. Shall we get back in the car?'

They sat in silence for a moment, with the rain hammering on the roof, while the demister and the heater worked overtime. Harry was certain that this was the right decision. It was what Molly would do.

'I just wanted to say, and please don't get the wrong idea, but you could stay at my place for the night. There's plenty of room. But I would quite understand – in the circumstances – I mean, me being a stranger, why you might not want to do that.'

'Well, I didn't think I was going to find a Good Samaritan so easily. You have a very trusting face and I probably should look for a hotel but I'm cold and miserable and your offer – your very gentlemanly offer

– is tempting. Thank you so much. My name's Alex, by the way'

'Harry, Harry Dymond. Right, let's go, shall we?'

As they made the ten-minute journey to Brélidy, Alex seemed to perk up very quickly, which Harry put down to her getting out of the cold and her relief at finding a bed for the night. But he quickly disentangled the image of Alex in a bed in his cottage. And the silence in the car was beginning to make the atmosphere slightly furtive. The only female who ever sat in the car with him was Molly but now, in the confined space, he was inhaling not the familiar scent of his wife but an altogether more sophisticated and evocative fragrance, which became enhanced as Alex unbuttoned her coat. Harry quickly turned the heater to zero and was relieved when the silence was broken.

'So, do you live here on your own?'

'No, it's just a holiday cottage. We've had it for about ten years.'

'We?'

'My wife and I. She didn't come over this time. She's looking… she wanted a bit of time to herself. I'm here just to shut it up for the winter, a few little jobs and the like.'

By the time Harry swung the car off the lane, the rain had eased and a rather limpid sun was glinting on the carpet of wet leaves that covered the drive. He reached over to the glove department to get the key and brushed Alex's knees, startling her. God, she must think I'm a dirty old man, he thought. He was glad to get inside the cottage and relieved to find the wood burner still alight.

'It's a gorgeous place. So quaint.' Alex was casting a long gaze around the living room, which also served as kitchen and diner. 'Lovely kitchen, too.'

As Harry stoked up the woodburner, he was feeling distinctly uncomfortable. Offering a woman a room for the night while standing in a windswept car park in Guingamp seemed quite a normal thing to do at the time. A bit of a gallant gesture actually. But seeing her standing in the small confines of his cottage – their cottage – made him feel uneasy. Harry's appraisal of a woman could be a little understated. He'd once shaken hands with the Princess of Wales when she visited his school to open a new science block and Molly couldn't wait to hear what he thought of her. 'Pleasant,' was Harry's considered opinion, 'very pleasant.'

But even he could see that Alex was a woman with a certain air about her: mid-fifties, he thought, but well-groomed; a blonde, sharp bob gave her a business-like air but her clothes - jeans, boots, scarf and gilet - suggested the more casual lifestyle of the Cotswolds. The thought of her sleeping here, even for a single night, even though she was upstairs and he down, now seemed distinctly inappropriate, even dangerous.

Alex seemed to be tuned in to Harry's misgivings and the fact that he was staring at her without speaking. Molly was always chastising him for this habit. 'Stop staring, Harry. People don't like being stared at.'

'Harry, I just wanted to say how much I appreciate you helping me out. But I don't want to get in your way or cause you any difficulties. If you'll show me where I'm sleeping, I'll be out of your hair and you can get on with your day.'

Harry realised that he was not being a very good host. He hadn't asked Alex to sit down, or shown her upstairs. Towels, would she need towels and soap? That's what Molly would do. And what else? Molly was always telling him that when people asked questions, they were not necessarily running a quiz or seeking specific information. It was often the precursor to opening up a conversation. 'Harry, if you just reply monosyllabically, nobody gets anywhere. Just look for the clues, Harry. Look for the clues.'

'Sorry, I'm not thinking. My wife is better at this than me. Let me show you upstairs and then I'll get you a towel and things. And you're not putting me out. It's the least I can do.'

With Alex in her bedroom, tidying herself up, Harry prepared lunch. Bread, ham and cheese was perfect, Alex had said. As he busied himself in the tiny kitchen, Harry felt more relaxed. This was going to be all right. Alex couldn't stay upstairs like someone in purdah. That was ridiculous. You just had to be grown up about these things. They'd have a bit of lunch and then perhaps, weather permitting, he would drive Alex to the coast. It was silly for her to miss the chance of seeing the sea. And this evening they could watch a film back in the cottage and then it would be time for bed. No, it would be fine. In the morning, Alex would be gone and his life would be back to normal.

At lunch, Harry essayed a little conversation and discovered that Alex was very happy to tell him about herself. She lived in Shepton Mallet and ran an antiques shop, although she was quick to point out that antiques was a bit too posh a word for the bric-a-brac she sold, most of which came from scouring the boot fairs, brocantes and depots vents of France, the object of this occasion's ill-fated trip. It was a living, she said, but she had to admit that she was getting too old for all the dashing about she did. Harry did not contradict her on this point, even when Alex paused for effect. She would love to be able to retire like Harry but that was some time off and in the circumstances she would have to continue working for some time.

'I'm a widow, you see,' she said, 'and my late husband, bless him, did not make provision for life without him.'

Harry realised that this called for a response. 'Married long, were you?'

'Actually no. About three years. He was my second husband; I divorced my first. Actually it's my little joke. I tell my friends that, with all the French trips I do, if I'd had a French husband in the middle of the other two and he'd been guillotined for murder, it would be like a scenario out of Henry VIII. Divorced, beheaded, died, etc.'

Alex laughed at her little joke, even though Harry continued eating his lunch impassively.

'That would be impossible,' he said. The guillotine hasn't been used for executions in France since 1977'

They were both glad to be in the car after lunch because it enabled them to converse in a less forced manner. Alex commented on the countryside, the quaint houses and, when they reached it, the stunning pink granite coast; Harry could discourse on the mound of information he had on the fauna, flora and history of Brittany. They stopped the car in Ploumanac'h, which was Molly's favourite haunt, a jumble of houses and shops surrounding a cove littered with the pink rocks that gave the coast its name. Alex said it was breathtaking, which Harry remembered was how Molly always described it. They had a coffee in a bar that nestled upon the beach and the low afternoon sun lit up the coral pink of the rocks, with their strange shapes that from different angles took on various human and animal forms.

'That rock looks like husband number one. He had that look on a bad day, which was usually every day. Is that a chateau of some sort on that outcrop further out?'

103

'That was built by the author of 'Quo Vadis?',' observed Harry. 'I believe he was Swiss,' he added, but he knew this to be true.

As they drove back to Brélidy, Alex nodded off and Harry was able to give her the occasional glance without her knowing. He watched her breasts rise and fall as she fell into a deep sleep and noticed that the tightness of her jeans betrayed a pair of shapely thighs.

'I'm sorry I fell asleep in the car,' she said later, 'after all the trouble you took to show me the sights.'

Harry was stoking up the woodburner again, normally the best part of the day for him. A time of settling down for the evening, a glass of beer to start, the wine already open, a couple of rom-coms set aside for viewing with Molly. Even though he rarely approved of her choice of film, he loved a cosy evening in the cottage with her, she thinking about the bar of chocolate that sat beckoningly at the back of the fridge, he contemplating the packet of cashews that Molly would not allow him at home because of his cholesterol but permitted him in France. But this evening there was another woman to share the evening with.

'Don't apologise,' he said. 'You've had quite a busy day and an eventful one, what with the breakdown and all. Is there a particular film that you'd like to see? Don't worry about me. I've seen them all, anyway. Sometimes twice.'

They watched *Sense And Sensibility*, which Alex hadn't seen and which Harry found tolerable. It was still quite early in the evening and he offered another film from the vast collection they had accumulated over the years.

'I don't mind just chatting for a bit, if that's OK with you. I love the atmosphere in this cottage. Do you mind if we don't have another film? Shall I do the honours?

Your glass looks like it needs refilling. Say when.' She leaned across him to fill his glass and he breathed in her fragrance once more. Harry had fired up the burner with cherry wood and the aroma of its smoky sap seemed to mingle in Harry's senses with Alex's sweet muskiness. It's just the wine making me a bit whoozy, he thought, as he gestured to her that his glass was full enough.

Harry began to feel slightly uncomfortable again. What was there to chat about? He already knew everything he wanted to know about Alex, who was now stretched out on the sofa, her long legs tucked beneath her. He knew he was required to say something, anything, to break the silence that was wafting around them like dry ice and threatening to cool the warm, soporific atmosphere that he was enjoying. Topics flicked across his consciousness like family photos viewed on a phone. The weather for the time of year (trite), the problem with the septic tank (boring), the absence of Molly (too personal), the War of the Breton Succession and its significance within the context of the Hundred Years' War (not enough time), the heave of Alex's bosom within the context of his relaxed demeanour (whoa, steady on now). But he knew that he needed to say something that centred on Alex herself. He cleared his throat noisily.

'Your visits to France,' he ventured, 'I mean you've spent quite a bit of time here. Bit of a Francophile at heart, eh?'

Alex did not throw back a quick response at such a lame opener. She took a sip of wine in a very studied manner and turned towards Harry with a half-smile.

'Yes, I do love France. I think I loved the country long before I ever visited. At school I wasn't brilliant academically but I had a flare for languages and French came easy to me. I remember the first time I opened my battered French textbook and saw how the language first concealed, then revealed a people so different from us but only twenty miles away across the Channel. I took to French like a canard to water. And then as a moody teenager I got into Sartre, Camus , Simone de Beauvoir, and all that existential stuff. While the girls at my school were fantasising about getting into the tartan trousers of the Bay City Rollers, I would be sitting on a bench affecting this conspicuous ennui while reading *L'Etranger*.'

'I could never understand that existential nonsense…'

'Anyway, that was just the beginning of my love affair with France because then I looked to earlier writers: Flaubert, de Maupassant, until I found what I was looking for, the genius of Zola. I've read everything Emile Zola ever produced and return to him time after time. The first time I visited France – it was on a school trip to Paris – I just felt that I was coming home. It's getting very warm in here. I think you've overdone the wood on the fire.'

Alex rose from the sofa and began pulling at her shirtfront and blowing down into her chest. She then moved to an armchair further away, settling herself in it like a contented cat.

'Well, that's me done. Now tell me about yourself,' she smiled. 'You seem quite a private person. You know, you don't give much away. I don't mean that as a criticism, by the way. You're the strong silent type, aren't you?'

I'd be less silent, he thought, if women didn't feel the need to do all the talking all of the time. In a different society I might be considered completely garrulous, the life, soul and wit of any gathering. It's all relative, you know.

'Nothing much to say, really. I taught, I paid additional pension contributions, I retired. That's where I am really. Glad to be out of it. I have a part-time job to keep me from going crazy and I really enjoy it. Yes, *really* enjoy it.'

Harry surprised himself by the force of the last remark because it was positively emotional for him. But he had to admit that he enjoyed his job, if not his colleagues. He explained that when he retired he thought that work was over for good for him. They were reasonably well off, the house paid for and the children settled. The first two years seemed to go well but it was Molly who noticed how restless he was becoming. If she returned five minutes later than normal from the optician's, Harry would be at the window watching for her car and complaining that her tea was getting cold.

'Harry, I don't want to be tied to a time set by you. You're a slave to it. The tea can wait. Sometimes, someone rings for an appointment just as I'm leaving or I might be chatting with the girls as we're locking up. Why don't you just leave everything until I appear at the door? Every time I come home from work, I find you anxious. Maybe you've got too much time on your hands.'

And it was Molly who suggested that Harry might apply to the museum for work as an attendant.

'You know how interesting you'd find all the exhibits, especially with your knowledge of everything under the sun. Who knows, you might find yourself in the art gallery. You love going in there, don't you?'

Of course, as with all Molly's suggestions, Harry dismissed this idea at first. But the next time he visited the museum, he enquired about vacancies. To his disappointment, they had none but he completed an application form and as luck would have it, he was called to interview about three weeks later. The summer season was coming up and the museum was looking for an attendant who could cover for holiday leave. The job was therefore only temporary but Harry didn't mind because he'd been allocated to the art gallery.

'So, which part of the gallery is the best to work in?' Alex enquired.

Harry didn't hesitate: 'The French Impressionists. Cardiff's got the finest collection outside London, you know.' Alex didn't know but in the next half hour she got the full history of the extensive collection of Impressionist paintings that the museum housed. If this was having a chat, Harry was enjoying it.

'So, tell me, which is your favourite painting in the collection? You must have a favourite.'

Harry did not have to think about this, because there was one painting that never failed to stir him. He couldn't really describe the feelings he got when he looked at the painting although they certainly weren't the feelings engendered by the purely artistic appreciation of an artist's skills, the feelings you get when you look at a Vermeer or a Caravaggio. But, nevertheless, they were feelings of great power and depth, of artistic achievement created in extremis.

'It's *Rain At Auvers* by Van Gogh.'

'They've got a Van Gogh in Cardiff?'

Harry sniffed and ignored the slightly veiled slur.

'It's one of three big canvases Vincent painted in the month that he died, July 1891. Vincent was at his lowest ebb at the time. I think everyone knows something about his troubled life. He thought he was failure. He'd sold only one painting in his career. He'd had a mental breakdown in Arles where he'd invited Gauguin to join him. Now Gauguin – he was Breton, by

108

the way - was an egotist by nature and not an easy person to rub along with and, of course, Vincent was having a breakdown. Not the best of situations, the two of them living in this small house in Arles, their evenings fuelled by alcohol. One night Vincent lost it. Gauguin thought he was intent on killing him but it was a cry for help. And then, of course, as everyone knows, Vincent lopped off a bit of his own ear. He was committed to the local asylum and eventually his brother, Theo, brought him back to Paris and lodged him in this little village called Auvers, where a Doctor Gachet was supposed to look after him. That was a bit of a laugh because Doctor Gachet probably needed his own psychiatrist. Anyway, Vincent's mental state did not improve. He wrote to his brother after he had painted these canvases that they expressed the extreme sadness and loneliness that he was feeling. A few days after finishing the paintings he shot himself but he botched the suicide attempt and lingered on a for a couple of days before he died.'

Harry finished speaking and realised that perhaps he had gone on a bit too much.

'You're a funny one, Harry,' said Alex. 'You're a very reserved guy but underneath you've got all your passions stirring away. Do you talk to Molly the way you've just talked to me?'

'Probably not…how did you know my wife's called Molly?'

'You must have mentioned it,' she replied, and then quickly 'Look, what I'm saying is that perhaps you keep yourself too buttoned up and that's not good for you. And maybe if you engaged more with Molly, she'd be out here with you now. Or have I touched upon a sore subject?'

Harry said nothing but rose and re-filled their glasses.

'I'm sorry, Harry. It's none of my business. But I sort of felt that you weren't happy with yourself. Forget I said anything.'

Harry felt that all this was too intrusive and coming from a stranger for whom he was doing a favour it was a bit of a cheek. He would be glad when tomorrow came and she was out of his hair. And yet Alex's intuition was right. But what could he do? He was no nearer to restoring his relationship with Molly and what if the space that she was seeking became more attractive than staying with him. Molly's temporary absence might become permanent if he was not careful.

'I know that I'm not easy to live with and I also know that the traits we're born with can become more obvious the older we get. When we were first together, Molly and I, she probably recognised that I had some funny ways, funny peculiar I mean, but women are very optimistic about their men folk. They think they can change them, mould them into another image and gradually strain out the bits they don't want. Men don't think like that. They meet a woman they fancy and think she's a bit of all right for whatever reasons and then they just settle down with her as she is. I do sort of know what I've become and I have to admit that I'm not unhappy with it. Perhaps it's the security blanket I need for the years ahead. Molly has never altered one jot. She's the girl I met at university and one of the great things about her is that she hasn't changed in the 40 years we've been together. Do you understand what I'm getting at?

'I think so. But the problem is not that you've changed or that parts of your personality have become somehow exaggerated over the years. It's all to do with where you go. Most women accept that their husbands are pretty hopeless in some departments. No, I'm not being rude. Get a group of women together and the first thing they'll talk about is their husbands and what a life they have with them. But it's mainly said in jest. What most women want is for their men to show a bit of sensitivity, a bit of empathy, from time to time. And I emphasise *from time to time* because women know that men are generally a lost cause. But it doesn't mean they don't love them any more.'

'But how do I do it? Change, I mean. I think I've lost the way.'

'There's no rulebook for this. You've just got look for opportunities to show Molly that you don't take her granted. Look at the way you been talking to me about Vincent. Why can't you talk to Molly like that? She'd feel your passion in the same way I do and once she knows that you've still got your emotions flowing under the surface, things will get better, I'm sure. But you've got to work at it, Harry. You've got to work at it.'

Harry actually managed a smile, which was the first in a long time. He even felt a wave of emotion rise in him so that he had to collect himself.

'Thank you,' he said. 'But I didn't mean to burden you with my problems.'

'You haven't. My only problem at the moment is that my body thinks it's undergoing sleep deprivation. I'm going to go up, if it's all right with you.'

Harry said he would finish his drink and watch the fire for a moment before turning in. He rose as she did and there was a hesitancy between them as if something was meant to happen. And then Alex moved fleetingly towards him and brushed his cheek with her lips.

'Thank you, Harry. It's been a lovely day.'

Harry listened below as she moved about upstairs. The fire cast a warm glow in the otherwise dark room.

111

Harry heard the upstairs toilet flush and the bedroom door close. His thoughts were all tangled up with the talk they had had together, which he had to admit made him feel so much better, with the wine he had consumed a little too hastily and with Alex upstairs, a woman undressing in his house, with no Molly present, with Brélidy fast asleep and with no one else in the world knowing or even bothering to know that an attractive woman was undressing and preparing to sleep a few metres above him, with all the possibilities that unfolded. It was a very piquant moment. He was not intending to do anything, of course, but the possibilities – the possibilities.

At that moment, he heard the bedroom door open. The landing light came on and Alex called to him to come up. As he rounded the turn in the stairs, he looked up at her standing above him, the light illuminating her body from behind so that he could see the shape of her outline, its roundness, even the gap between her parted legs.

'I'm really sorry, Harry, but there's a spider in my room. I can't stand spiders.'

Harry squeezed past her in the narrow stairwell, catching her scent again and brushing against her breasts. He dealt with the spider by flushing it down the toilet in the bathroom and then had to squeeze past Alex once more as she waited on the landing.

'My hero,' she said with a mock damsel air.

Harry paused and placed his hand upon Alex's breast, gently, as if he was admiring the contours of a Rodin nude. Alex did not move, did not attempt to move his hand but said softly though firmly:

'Harry, I'm flattered by the gesture but this would make things very complicated between us. Maybe you should finish your drink and go to bed. Good night.'

Dear Leonard,

Oh my God! What was I thinking of? I must be crazy. What if she had been willing? To think that I could have had sex with a complete stranger here, in this cottage, our cottage. I've been married for 40 years and I've never even thought about another woman in that way. Is being unfaithful that easy?

I don't know what came over me. Inviting Alex to stay the night here seemed quite natural but, as this evening wore on, being in such close confines with her, just the two of us, was different. I know I've drunk a fair bit this evening and I admit that I was imagining Alex undressing upstairs but that's harmless stuff, isn't it? It was seeing her at the top of the stairs that did it; I could see the curves of her body and she made no attempt to cover herself. I thought that she was offering herself to me. But that's no excuse , is it?

When I met her this morning, it wouldn't have occurred to me to treat her as a sex object. She looked a bit bedraggled and frankly quite plain but this evening I must say she looked very attractive and I enjoyed her company. I felt myself being drawn to her and not just physically. She has a lot about her. She's more outgoing and sophisticated, yes that's it, more sophisticated than Molly. MOLLY! Oh my God! What is Molly going to think about this? I've been unfaithful in mind and deed, if you consider groping another woman's breast as unfaithful. Do you think that counts as unfaithful, Leonard?

Of course, Molly won't know because I can't possibly tell her. But what if I look guilty? And should I tell her about meeting Alex? *Oh, by the way, Molly, I let a woman stay the night in the cottage. She had nowhere to stay and I was just being gallant. What was she like?*

113

Eh, very plain, very plain indeed, with a squint and a face full of warts. Molly would see straightaway that I was lying. I can never hide anything from her.

Leonard, I've wandered into very dangerous territory here and made a bloody fool of myself. And how am I going to face Alex in the morning? She said I was too self-contained to let someone in. I don't know what this means. All I know is that I deviated from my normal sense of ordered existence. I did something that I wouldn't dream of doing and whenever I've done that in the past something terrible has happened. I think that's why I build a wall of habit and certainty around me. It's tedious even to me sometimes and extremely irritating to others and I don't really know why I do it but I do. It's like a fortress in which my emotions are under siege but with luck I keep my enemies at bay. But this evening Alex was like a fifth columnist who had infiltrated my domain, or some kind of Mata Hari who used her wiles to get deep into my psyche and undermined the inhibitions that normally keep me safe and in control.

Whatever I am and whatever Molly and I have become, I cannot face being without her. But tonight I put all that in jeopardy, in one unbelievably base and stupid action. It's like watching in slow motion as a precious object falls from your grasp and crashes to the floor in a thousand pieces and you know in a split second that the clock can't be turned back to allow you to hold it more carefully.

What am I going to do, Leonard? You've got to help me here.

CHAPTER 12

Harry rose early after a fitful night and busied himself in the kitchen, clearing up from last night, his ear attuned to any sounds coming from upstairs. He put on a pot of coffee and popped some croissants in the oven to warm through. The flush of the toilet upstairs told him that Alex would soon appear. He already had the words sorted out in his mind. When Alex appeared, she had her coat on and headed straight for the door.

'I'm going to walk up the lane to get a signal. I need to check with the garage that my car is ready.' And she was gone, leaving Harry open-mouthed, with the coffee pot in mid-pour.

Harry spent a few more minutes fussing in the kitchen, endlessly wiping every surface, until Alex opened the door and headed for the stairs, her cheeks slightly flushed by the brisk walk in the cool November air.

'Alex, just wait a minute, please. About last night, I'm really sorry. I mis-read the situation. I don't want you to think I'm …'

'A letch? You don't want me to think you're a dirty old man. And, Harry, there was no situation to mis-read. Anyway, forget it. You're not the first man to think a widow is up for it just because she shows an interest in a man.'

'That's why I feel so bad. I tried to take advantage of you. I really am sorry.'

Alex paused and turned to look at the neatly laid breakfast table.

'Look,' said Harry, 'let's have a nice breakfast and then you can be on your way. I'll make you something to eat for the ferry, just in case you get hungry.'

'That's the bad news, Harry. The garage didn't get the part yesterday, so they couldn't work on my car. They have it there now but the car won't be ready for me to get the afternoon ferry from Roscoff. You're stuck with me for another day, I'm afraid.'

Harry tried to collect his thoughts, while Alex continued.

'If you want to make amends for last night, you can do me a favour. I was banking on catching the ferry to Plymouth today because I have to deliver a parcel to a friend there. There's no ferry to Plymouth tomorrow and my only chance of getting back is to get a ferry via Cherbourg or St Malo, and they both go to Portsmouth. I don't fancy having to make a detour from Portsmouth to Plymouth to deliver the parcel and then have to trek all the way up the M5 to Shepton Mallet. Would you deliver the parcel in Plymouth if I sort out the arrangements? You're going Roscoff-Plymouth aren't you?'

It was the least he could do in the circumstances and it would make a potentially embarrassing extra day with Alex more bearable.

'Where does this chap live?' asked Harry, hoping that he didn't have to go too far out of his way.

'If I call him, he'll meet you at the Hoe, by Drake's statue. He'll be in a silver grey Jaguar. His name is Ben'

Harry thought that this was beginning to sound a bit cloak and dagger. What was so precious about this parcel that they had to be so furtive?

'Okay, Harry, let me explain. My friend collects 19th century French erotica. You know, sepia-tinted images of plump ladies in the buff and some a little bit more risqué. Each to his own, I say. I don't judge. I have a contact in Rennes who deals in this sort of stuff. It's all fairly tame by today's standards but it's also very saleable. It's a small sideline for me and it's all perfectly legal. If my friend wants to get off on this stuff when he could just as easily go and buy a dirty mag in his local newsagent, that's his business.'

But why couldn't Harry just meet him at the port, once he had cleared passport control? Alex gave a long sigh as if she was beginning to lose patience with him.

'My friend is a well-known local businessman – you know, Masonic lodge and all that. He doesn't want to be seen parked in the port, collecting porn from someone who's just got off the ferry. He wants to do it more discreetly, shall we say. Does that make sense to you?'

Of course, Harry had to agree and there wasn't any real harm in it, was there?

~

With breakfast finished, Alex went for a walk outside. Harry was feeling better about things. After all, she had been very good about what had happened last night, very gracious in the circumstances. Glancing through the window he could see her standing by the shrine deep in thought. The day was looking more promising; the wind had dropped and the clouds were scattering to reveal a sky of cornflower blue. Taking his courage in both hands, Harry walked outside and crossed the lane to where Alex was standing. She heard the crunch of his shoes on the dry leaves that lay in drifts all over the lane. She had a handful of chestnuts, which she held out before her as if making some kind of votive offering.

'Are these the ones you can roast and eat?'

117

'Yes, said Harry, 'but you have to make a cut in them, otherwise they explode. Molly and I tried roasting some on the fire once but we forgot to cut them. We spent the whole evening dodging them – they were going off like a machine gun.'

Alex laughed and Harry felt relief at the return to some kind of normality between them. He would take whatever would make this final day bearable.

'So, what's the history of this shrine?' she asked. 'I imagine you know all about it.' She said this with only the slightest hint of irony in her voice, as if she was mildly interested.

'It's dedicated to Saint Columban. He was an Irish monk who brought Christianity to these parts in the sixth century. The church in the village is also dedicated to him. There are loads of shrines in Brittany and they all claim their waters have some form of healing power. This one was supposed to cure illnesses of the mind and on the saint's holy day people would flock here to take a cure. I'm thinking of trying it out myself.'

'Good. Now you're poking fun at yourself; that's a good start to self-improvement but, if you're looking for a miracle, you might need several immersions. As Zola said: *The road to Lourdes is littered with crutches, but not one wooden leg,'*

She gazed at his sad, puzzled face, and gently, with no hint of sensuality, touched his arm.

'Harry, I'm having a little joke at your expense. I'm just saying that you have to work at it.'

Alex offered to take Harry for lunch. It would be her treat after all the inconvenience she had caused and she would take no ifs or buts. They drove into Tréguier and parked in the town square, close to the seated statue of the anticlerical Ernest Renan who threatens to wave his stout cane at any worshippers entering the cathedral opposite. Harry recommended the Auberge de Trégor, which was just a few steps away. The restaurant had few customers and they were ushered to a table for two close to the granite fireplace where a fire had been lit, even though it was quite a mild day outside. The owner pointed out that the *formule* was not available as it was a public holiday in France. Harry scratched his head and realised that it was Armistice Day. He felt bad about Alex having to pay for the a la carte menu and was happy to go halves but she said it was her treat.

At the table behind sat three Brits who talked loudly throughout the meal. Harry had his back to them and so Alex had to explain in whispers what they looked like. It became a little game between them throughout the course of the meal. Alex observed that the trio consisted of a middle-aged couple and a younger male companion who was intent on impressing them with his knowledge, which was mainly about the mysteries of the past. He seemed to be obsessed by how the pyramids could have been built by a culture that only had bronze implements. How did they dress all that stone when they didn't have iron or steel? If the couple were minded to offer an answer to this and all the other questions he posed, he was quick to answer his own question and, before they could comment on that, pose another. What about the Yazca Lines in the Peruvian desert? What about Stonehenge? Harry began to get agitated and threatened to turn around and put him in his place but Alex laid her hand upon his arm and said hold your horses, they're about to leave. The trio eventually fussed themselves into coats and scarves, thanked madame for a delightful meal and finally left the restaurant. Madame came over to his table to replenish the carafe of water and Alex in perfect French asked her whether she had enjoyed the history lesson from the next table. Madame laughed at this and shrugged her shoulders.

Harry was pleased that the meal was going well, that the embarrassment of last night was apparently forgotten. Alex was such an accomplished person, he thought, with a delicacy of manner and bearing – the way she sipped her wine or dabbed her lips with her napkin - that made her extremely attractive. He immediately pulled himself up on this last observation because that was not what this meal was all about. It was about starting off on the right foot again.

On the way back to the cottage, before they lost the mobile signal down in the dell, Alex phoned the garage again. The car would be ready by the end of the day, she said, but because of the inconvenience of the delay they would bring it to the cottage at 8.30am sharp tomorrow. That's unusual customer service from the French, observed Harry. Alex said that it was all a matter of how you buttered them up and French garage owners were suckers for a bit of English charm. She told Harry not to worry about seeing her off in the morning. She'd pack everything tonight and leave when the car was delivered because it was a long drive to Cherbourg for the afternoon ferry.

Dear Leonard,

Today went better than I deserved, Leonard. Alex and I seem to have restored some sense of normality, which is more than you could expect after you have groped your house guest. Alex has been more than gracious about the whole thing and I'm very relieved, I can tell you. And thankfully she will be gone tomorrow morning and our paths will not cross again.

Mind you, the only fly in the ointment is having to deliver this rather dubious package to this chap in Plymouth. It's all a bit murky if you ask me – furtive meetings in car parks and all that. I hope he doesn't think I'm connected in any way with this trade in vintage erotica. I mean I'm a perfectly normal man with the same needs as the next. What I'm saying is I'm no prude.

When I was a boy my mother used to clean for a middle-aged bloke in Bideford, Mr Goodman his name was. She also did all his washing and ironing. Sometimes in the school holidays she'd take me with her because otherwise I'd be on my own at home. My sister was always out with her girl friends but I never had much company. I liked going there with my mother because it was so different from my house. For one thing it was always spotlessly tidy and that wasn't just on account of my mother's cleaning. When you arrived it was clean and tidy, with everything ordered and in its place. Our house wasn't dirty as such but it was just chaotic. No one ever put anything away and if they did it meant stuffing things under seat cushions or behind chairs. I hated it.

But this man's house was like something you saw in magazines: wall-to-wall carpets, a serving hatch and a reproduction of Tretchikoff's bilious Chinese lady. My mother didn't like me wandering around the house when she was there. I had to sit in the lounge with a book, with strict instructions not to touch anything. But one day when we were at the house, Mr Goodman had left a note asking if she'd get in some milk and bread for him. So she popped out to the shops leaving me on my own. My mother would never let me venture upstairs but I was curious to see what it was like. I knew I had at least twenty minutes to spare before she came back, so up I went. There were two bedrooms, which of course were immaculate, and a bathroom with a pink suite, which blew my mind. But what really impressed me was the furniture, all dark polished wood and matching pieces, not like the mismatch of stuff that inhabited our house. The second bedroom doubled as an office with a large bureau at one end. I pulled down the lid of it and stared at the leather-covered desk that it became, with all the compartments filled so neatly with papers, letters and pens. It was an Aladdin's cave to me. And then right at the back of one of the compartments I spotted a key. My curiosity got the better of me and I tried it in various drawers of the bureau until the bottom one slid open. I knew my mother would be back in about five minutes but I had time.

The drawer opened to reveal a pile of magazines, most of which had men on their covers, men in bathing trunks or pouches posing like Charles Atlas. Inside were similar pictures of half-naked men, on the beach, astride motorbikes, sometimes wrestling playfully with each other; you get the message, I'm sure. But I didn't get it at all. They were just men to me. I looked further under the pile of magazines, where there were loose, dog-eared photographs of undressed men but these weren't posing. Oh dear me, no. I don't need to paint a picture, do I? I was dumbstruck. I didn't know much about any form of sex and what I saw there just

122

shocked and confused me. Boys in school would talk about what you had to do with girls and I didn't grasp much of what they said. But this was something that had never entered my mind. Well, didn't Queen Victoria refuse to believe that lesbians existed?

In a panic I pushed the magazines back in the drawer, locked it up and put everything back in order. I raced downstairs and dived onto a chair in the lounge, picking up my book as I did, just as my mother was opening the door. She was muttering about having bought some nice cakes to have with a cup of tea. She looked into the lounge as she was taking off her coat and gave me a long, hard look. I must have looked flushed or something because she asked me if I was all right. She never said anything at the time but a couple of weeks later she was really busy and as my sister was going into Bideford she asked her to drop off Mr Goodman's ironing. But my sister forgot to take it with her and so I volunteered. It was only one bus ride and a short walk but my mother nearly bit my head off. She said very sharply that she would take it herself.

Mr Goodman was what people in those days called a 'confirmed bachelor' and those magazines no doubt satisfied a need. So I shouldn't judge the persons to whom the package is directed. I just wish the whole thing wasn't so furtive.

CHAPTER 13

The next day Harry was up by eight o'clock to make sure Alex had at least a cup of coffee before she left. It was chilly in the living room and, and not wishing to set a roaring fire so early in the day, he switched on the electric heaters to warm up the room before she appeared. As he waited for the water to boil he looked out through the panes of the front door towards the shrine, which was obscured by a shroud of damp mist that hung in the still air. That's in for day, he thought. No sounds came from upstairs and time was getting on if Alex wanted to be ready when her car was delivered. Perhaps she had overslept. Should he call up to her? He certainly didn't want to go upstairs. He then noticed that the key, which was normally kept on the windowsill, was in the door. He tried it and it opened. Alex had gone without saying goodbye, which puzzled him.

With the 'incident' now consigned to history, they had spent a pleasant enough evening chuckling away while viewing compilations of various classic sitcoms culled from Sunday newspaper giveaways. Harry had felt more relaxed in her company. Alex drank very little – as she kept saying, it was a long drive to Cherbourg – but she kept filling Harry's glass, so that he found himself staggering to bed and succumbed to a very deep and heavy sleep. Maybe she had tried to wake him before she left but he was still dead to the world.

Then Harry noticed the parcel. It was sitting, brooding, on the dining table where Alex had obviously left it. Wrapped in brown paper, it was much bigger than he'd thought it would be and it made him wonder how large an appetite someone needed for Victorian porn. He was tempted to slit open the wrapping paper to get at the box that was lurking beneath, just out of curiosity you understand, but there was so much gaffer tape securing the parcel that he knew that however careful he was it would always look as if it had been tampered with. He traced his fingers over the brown wrapping paper and felt the contours of the box underneath, but he decided he had no need of such titillation and would confine his lusts to fantasies of Katherine Jenkins knocking on his door one night, soaked to the skin, asking if she could borrow a cup of sugar. He put the parcel in the cupboard under the stairs.

Harry set himself tasks to fill up the one full day he still had left before returning home. He spent the morning giving a lick of white emulsion to those parts of the walls that needed going over after a season of visitors. It was dry enough to mow the front lawn again, which took longer than he thought but before the afternoon dimmed into its November gloom he still had enough time to spray the brambles behind the cottage, to weaken their number and at least give himself a slight advantage before they launched their spring offensive and continued their slow, indomitable onslaught in their mission to erase the cottage from the face of the earth.

His final task was to raid his woodpile, gathering the logs in his arms to stock up the log basket. The day had remained cold and as the light faded outside, he could feel a keener autumnal chill begin to grip his shoulders.

By six o'clock the woodburner was pumping the heat around the room, a chicken casserole was simmering on the hob and, having decided that the sun was well over the yardarm, he had a glass of Pelforth at his elbow. He had finished the novel he was reading and it was too early to watch a DVD, so he picked up the guest book that visitors were encouraged to fill during their stays. Their comments regularly popped up on the cottage website because in truth rarely were there any negative remarks. If the weather was good, the comments were inevitably about the delights of the pink granite coast and the quaint towns and villages. If the summer weather had been unkind, then visitors spoke favourably about the cottage's charms.

Bizarrely, one year a visitor had sought fit to comment on the films that they had watched. Obviously, bad weather had forced them to spend too much time indoors. However, their remarks extended to reviewing the plots of the various movies they had seen and there were conclusions such as 'disappointing ending' and 'implausible storyline'. Molly had taken offence at this on the grounds that it amounted to a veiled criticism of the quality of the films that she and Harry provided.

This season's comments were par for the course. It had been a warm summer and the comments of guests centred upon outdoor excursions to the many beaches, restaurants and sights to which families had trekked. The directors of *Titanic*, *Gladiator* and *Carry On Camping* could sleep easy in their beds. He read through the comments month by month. They tailed off in September because bookings were less frequent and there was only one in October, the last of the season. Harry read it with interest and was intrigued. He couldn't understand why but it needed a second look, so he closed the guest book and packed it away in his luggage.

The next day was Harry's last and an afternoon ferry meant a midday getaway from the cottage. He loaded the car with enough wine to see him into the New Year

126

and made sure the mysterious parcel was accessible on top, although he covered it with a fleece. Shutting the tailgate, he counted in his head the final tasks to be done - turn off the water, put down some mouse poison and put up the shutters. He had plenty of time in hand for the drive to Roscoff. It was a clear day and the sun, though low in the sky, was casting its light upon the haphazard rows of irregular stones that made up the main wall of the cottage. Harry had time to sit on the front step with a cup of coffee and just relax for half an hour before departing. Sitting in the sunshine, he was a little peeved that the whole business with Alex had robbed him of the quietude that this place normally afforded him. He loved nothing more than just to sit outside, perhaps reading, but more often than not just sitting. Molly liked to enjoy herself by bustling about inside, moving things around and adding the little touches that she thought appealed to guests - a new cushion here, a vase moved there, a different picture for the wall, a new gadget in the kitchen. He used to complain to her when he came back indoors and found the whole place transformed but if he was honest he quite liked the contrast of him relaxing while she was a hive of activity just within earshot. Couples can grow closer even when the things they're doing are poles apart, so long as they're doing them in a kind of togetherness. Perhaps he could have been more complimentary to Molly about her efforts to make the place look attractive. He glanced behind him as if to see if Molly was even now re-arranging the objects on the dresser and was overcome with a feeling of emptiness. *Next time I will say how nice it all looks.*

No time for sad thoughts. He must enjoy these last moments, just sitting here. He liked to imagine that previous occupants did the same, gnarled Breton peasants scraping their wooden sabots on the steps as they took the weight off their aching bones after a day in the fields or maybe just to get out of the smoky cottage with its earth floor and rough-hewn furniture, while waiting for a pot of meagre stew to cook on the fire. Whoever had built this cottage hundreds of years ago had taken advantage of an outcrop of rock, which emerged out of a high, curved bank, by using it as one of the gable ends of the cottage itself. Perhaps it was the economy of necessity but the rock was going nowhere, so why not use it as a ready-made wall? It was possible to climb up the rock (though Harry only ever did it this when Molly was pre-occupied inside) and stand level with the roof and just below the chimney. Harry liked the thought of the cottage bracing itself against the strength of the rock as he was now bracing his back against the jamb of the doorway – his body, the house and the rock all rooted into the Breton soil.

It was such a pity that this trip had offered him so little pleasure, what with Molly being absent. He did not want to come alone again. But for the moment he would just make the most of these precious few minutes. As he felt the weak autumn sunshine reflect off the stone wall and gather itself around his shoulders, his breathing slowed and his muscles relaxed. He closed his eyes. The only sounds he could hear were the singing of the birds, the rustle of the wind through the trees, and, if he listened really hard, the trickling of the stream that bounded the property. This morning seemed even quieter and, as he sat on the steps, there occurred a strange pause as just for a few moments every sound ceased. The natural world around him in that small corner of Brittany seemed to return to its factory settings for just a tiny gap in time, in the same way as a group of friends around a dining table cease their chatterings or draw breath at exactly the same time so that an awkward and unexpected silence envelopes them and someone has to quickly break the spell by saying something, anything, to restart the conversation. But Harry had no wish to break this spell as the birdsong stopped, the murmur of the soft breeze died and even the brook was stilled. It was like the dawn of the world when a tree could crash silently in the forest because its sound waves could find no human ear. The only sounds that Harry could hear were his own breathing and the vibration of his tinnitus inside his head.

The silence surrounded him with questions. What happens now, Harry? *I don't know.* Can you go back and continue as you were? *Probably not.* Do you want things to be different? *I want them to be better.* In what way? *I think I have taken Molly for granted and I want things to be better between us.* How will this come about? *I suppose it has to come from me.* Can you change? *I don't know but I have to try.*

A gust of wind came down the lane, sending a shower of chestnut leaves whirling to the ground, as the song of a blackbird reminded its neighbours that there are always territorial boundaries to respect.

~

Out of courtesy Harry knew that he would have to say goodbye to Guillaume and Sylvie until his (and hopefully Molly's) return in the spring. Rather than walk over to their house and then come back for the car, he drove the few hundred yards over the bridge and up to their house, the springs of the overloaded vehicle groaning over the rutted driveway. A plume of smoke from the chimney and two parked cars showed that they were at home. The crunch of Harry's tyres on the gravel alerted Guillaume who came out of the house first, followed by Sylvie. The couple waited uneasily as Harry approached. Normally there was a firm handshake from Guillaume and four pecks from Sylvie, but they did not come forward to greet Harry. Even he checked his steps.

'I'm off to the ferry. Just wanted to say cheerio and we'll see you in the new year.'

'You will come alone again?' asked Guillaume snootily.

'No, of course not. Molly will be with me.'

'Send our love to Molly and tell her we miss her very much,' said Sylvie. 'We hope that we will see her again.'

'Of course, you will,' replied Harry, wondering if it was just the language barrier getting in the way. Perhaps they've had a row, he thought, or I've come at a tricky moment. Deciding that retreat was the best option, he gave a nondescript wave and got back into the car. As he pulled up the drive, he could see Guillaume and Sylvie in his rear-view mirror, still staring after him as he turned into the lane and climbed the hill.

The crossing from Roscoff to Plymouth was uneventful. The sea was unusually calm for the time of year and Harry was able to get a good long sleep in his cabin. The boat docked promptly at 9.30pm and Harry was relieved to find that disembarkment was very quick, owing to the small number of cars on board. He exited the port and followed the signs for the Hoe. Drake's monument loomed ahead as he slowed the car and strained to see the outline of a Jaguar. Suddenly a pair of headlights flashed on the left hand side and Harry swung his car in their direction. It was a Jaguar all right. Parking alongside it, he wondered what next to do because the Jaguar's occupant made no move to get out. Perhaps I should make the first move, he thought. He got out, lifted the tailgate and removed the parcel from the rear. Still no movement from the Jaguar. Walking around to the driver's side of the car, he could make out a man's shape, head down with his hands on the steering wheel. He was about to tap on the windscreen when a rear window wound down and a hand, eerily disembodied in the darkness, emerged from the back. 'Give me the parcel, Harry. I haven't got all night.'

Harry was about to protest at the obvious lack of courtesy but before he could say anything, the hand grabbed the parcel and as suddenly as this happened the whole area was lit up with headlights. The Jaguar roared into life and with a screech of wheel spin sped off, the hand still extended, only to be blocked by two cars, out of which tumbled three or four men who quickly surrounded the car, ripped open the doors and grabbed the occupants. All this happened in seconds and Harry was just wondering what he should do in such a strange and unforeseen situation as this, when two hands were laid on his shoulders and a voice whispered in his ear: 'OK, mate, you're under arrest.'

~

The interview room at the police station was not as Harry expected it to be, accustomed as he was to TV police dramas in which the suspect usually faced the police officers across a bare table in a spartan room decorated in battleship grey. This room was actually quite comfortable in a utilitarian sort of way: carpet, upholstered chairs and even a couple of touristy seascapes decorating the walls.

Having given a statement, he was waiting for the officer to return, no doubt having consulted a superior on the story he had told. He was not unduly concerned by the turn of events. True, being arrested and bundled into a police car was scary at the time but his main concern was for Molly who was expecting him home. He had been allowed a phone call to her and was a little ashamed at having to concoct a story about dislodging his exhaust coming off the ferry and having to stay over in a B&B until he could sort out a repair tomorrow, but he didn't want to tell her the truth just now. Telling Molly that he was under arrest for trafficking in illegal goods would panic her and, anyway, this whole business would soon be sorted once the police saw that the 'goods' were only a bit of Victorian soft porn. Clearly they thought the parcel contained drugs or some such stuff. Matters weren't helped by that chap Ben trying to escape. It made it all so much worse. No doubt his reputation was down the swannee when the press got hold of the news: 'Prominent local business man caught red handed with pornography.' Surely the police would soon realise that Harry had done nothing wrong but why were they taking so long about it?

Detective Sergeant Wilkins came back into the room with what looked like Harry's statement in one hand and a coffee cup in the other. He had a world-weary air about him but, since it was now well past midnight, Harry could readily sympathise with how he must be feeling, with all the other problems that Plymouth on a Saturday night was likely to produce.

'So, Harry, let's run through your story again, if you don't mind. You meet a stranger in France who asks you to carry a parcel for her across the Channel and deliver it to a person, another stranger, and the handover is to take place in a secluded car park at night. Have I got that right?'

Harry detected a slight edge to the policemen's voice, in contrast to his earlier more affable demeanour. Good

132

cop, bad cop, in one personification perhaps? He also felt that he might have underestimated Wilkins somewhat because, although what he was saying was true, his summing up of the events surrounding Harry's arrest was now slanted towards a more devious interpretation of his actions and motive.

Harry swallowed hard. 'As a bare statement of the facts, yes, but as I said earlier the lady in question wasn't able to get a ferry to Plymouth where she was due to meet up with this chap. I was just helping her out. I couldn't see any harm in it.'

'Tell me about this 'lady' again. What is your relationship with her? How long have you known her'

'As I've said, I only met her this week. Her car had broken down, she stayed with me for a couple of days while it was being fixed and then she returned to the UK, leaving me with the parcel which she could no longer deliver in person.'

'Why did she not stay in a hotel while her car was being repaired? Isn't it a bit odd that you let this 'lady' stay with you, when you don't know anything about her? You were taking a bit of a risk weren't you? And I asked about your relationship.'

'There was none. There is none. What are you implying?'

'I'm not implying anything. But isn't it strange that you meet someone for the first time, apparently innocently, and then agree to handle illegal goods, which she supplies you.'

'What do you mean 'illegal' goods. There wasn't anything illegal in the parcel; of dubious taste maybe, but not illegal.'

'You had sight of the goods you were delivering?'

'No, but surely dirty pictures and old ones at that are not illegal.'

'Harry, if the parcel contained what you claim it contained, do you think you'd still be here? It wasn't dirty pictures. Otherwise, we'd be arresting every Tom, Dick and – sorry, Harry – who had a copy of Playboy in his luggage. OK, let me tell you what was in the parcel. Harry, have you ever heard of tome raiders?'

Harry screwed up his face like a small boy who doesn't know the answer to an obvious question.

'There's a lucrative trade in antique books and maps, sometimes stolen to order. Collectors will pay high prices for this sort of stuff and dealers, who often pass themselves as reputable booksellers or antique dealers, will ignore where they've come from. Only a couple of years ago, this chap - ex-Cambridge University to boot - was jailed for stealing over one million pounds worth of books.'

'But where are they stolen from?'

'Libraries mostly, you know university libraries with so many books on dusty shelves, books that haven't been catalogued for decades, with systems that are antiquated and with staff that are doddery or bent or both. That's what was in the parcel, Harry. And they can be a nice little earner, whether it's maps or books. There was this American guy who stole hundreds of rare maps worth over 500,000 dollars from libraries across the country. He'd seen how the market for antique maps had become very lucrative and he didn't care about splitting open rare books in order to extract individual maps and pages. Imagine that, Harry, a rare and precious volume, preserved for centuries, just ripped apart for the one or two maps in contained. And the sad thing is that some libraries are reluctant to report any theft because they're afraid that the donations they receive will dry up if anything got out.'

Harry felt like a poker player whose full house has just been trumped by a royal flush and his opponent is now greedily sweeping the pile of money to his end of the table.

'We've been liaising with police on the continent for a while now. We had a tip off that the gang was using the Channel ferries, where security can be a bit lax. I mean who wants to strip every car down to the metal when most people using the ferries from France are just normal Brits who are coming back off holiday. The man you gave the parcel to is a local antiques dealer who we've suspected for a long time was doing a bit of fencing on the side. You handed him maps and books that would probably fetch about £30,000'

Harry's mouth suddenly felt very dry and he looked longingly at the coffee cup that Wilkins was putting to his lips.

'Let's get back to the lady in question. You say you don't know her, you have no relationship with her. Do you expect me to believe that? Come on, Harry, we're men of the world. You're alone in a cottage with a woman who's ten years younger than you. Nobody knows she's there and nobody's going to know, least of all your wife. Did she ask you to deliver the parcel in return for – what shall we call it – services rendered?'

'How dare you suggest…'

'No, let me finish, because the alternative scenario is that you must be the most naïve and gullible person I've ever come across.'

Harry didn't like either of Wilkins's theories but he was beginning to think he fitted the second one very neatly. He had to admit that the whole episode looked very fishy indeed but the truth was that he had merely delivered the parcel to save her the trouble of a long detour.

'So, you've never visited her antiques shop in Shepton Mallet.'

'No, and I don't intend to.'

'You'd have a job, Harry, because it doesn't exist and in a sense neither does she. We can find no trace of an Alexandra Boyd running an antiques business in Shepton Mallet or anywhere else for that matter. So now we have you acting as a courier delivering illegal goods for a woman who is using an alias. People don't normally use aliases unless they've got something to hide. So, doing what you did for someone who's not what she says she is... well, that's not very clever, is it Harry? So, tell me why we shouldn't charge you with handling stolen goods?'

Harry sat there dumbfounded. This was not working out as he'd thought. A cup of tea and *Sorry, Mr Dymond, there's been a misunderstanding. You're free to go* was clearly no longer on the cards. Detective Sergeant Wilkins sat back in his chair, his hands clasping the back of his head, the smile of satisfaction on his face saying game, set and match.

Harry was trying to dig deep but with great difficulty. He had to find something in the swirl of facts that were filling his brain. Had he really been duped by Alex, played for a mug, fooled by a woman into committing a crime? And now it was inevitable that Molly would find out and, worse than the crime into which he had been snared, would be the accusation that he had had some sort of liaison with a femme fatale. He was finished, finished for good. In the middle of the swirling facts, buzzing around his brain, was a phrase that he had once known and actually taught to pimply fifth-formers in another time when he dabbled in other subjects, subsidiary to history. What was that phrase? It was almost in his grasp and his mind strained to clutch it as it drifted around his consciousness.

'Mens rea… I don't have mens rea,' Harry mumbled to himself.

Wilkins leaned forward, unclasping his hands and placing them on the table. 'What did you say?'

'When I first started teaching, I had a gap in my timetable and the Head persuaded me to fill it by teaching an 'O' level called Principles of English Law. It was an option offered to pupils who were struggling to find another subject to study. I said I'd do it, otherwise I wouldn't have had a full timetable and my wife was expecting our first child. Couldn't afford a cut in salary at that time…'

'…Harry, what has all this got to do…?'

'Please, let me finish. I'm trying to collect my thoughts. There were two principles that had to be present to constitute a crime. No, that's not completely true, because – I remember now – some crimes could be strict liability but I'm digressing. Generally, a crime has two components – mens rea and actus reus. The actus reus is the physical nature of a crime, all the material facts and circumstances that constitute the illegal act. Yes, it's all coming back to me now. I can see that I did the actus reus. I mean I handled or carried illegal goods. I did the physical part that makes it a crime. But a crime has to have a mental element, the mens rea, the intention of the criminal to commit the actus reus. You can prove that I did the act but, and I say this with all due respect, I don't think you can prove that I had the knowledge, intention, or thoughts to *do* that act. I seem to have been very stupid in agreeing to do what I did but I didn't intend to commit a crime. I think that when the Crown Prosecution Service –

they're the ones who do the prosecution, don't they? – I think they'll look at me, a retired and somewhat pathetic sixty-two-year-old ex-teacher, who's got an unblemished past with not even a parking ticket to his name, and they'll say that this guy has got to be so stupid to be duped by a woman that his story has got to be true. She used her feminine charms and he fell for it, hook, line and stupid bloody sinker. He actually believed that he was just delivering some porn to some equally pathetic bloke. They'll say it's so stupid, it's got to be true and we can't be bothered wasting public money to get a conviction on him when we've got the guy who actually received the goods.'

Harry swallowed hard and stared red-eyed at Wilkins.

'Do you think I could have a cup of tea...please?'

Dear Leonard,

It was past five am when they released me without charge. I could have got back into the car and headed straight up the A30 to get away from Plymouth and my shame. But I knew that arriving home in the early hours would not help the story I'd already told Molly. So I wandered down to the seafront in the hope that I might find an all-night cafe to get something to eat and drink but of course it was all shut. I felt so low, Leonard. It was that time of the night, I think you know it well, the desperate hours, when people are at their most vulnerable, when despair squeezes the very life and soul out of you and you can contemplate things that would normally never enter your mind.

I didn't realise I was that far gone. I couldn't tell you if I was actually thinking of, you know, doing anything silly. I just felt so lonely, Leonard. I felt that I was outside the real world. I was a lost soul whom no one cared for. I was insignificant. The world could go on without me and would probably be the better for it.

I went down to the sea itself. It was still quite dark but you could see that the dawn was just about to break. The sea was calm but still relentlessly throwing itself on the shore making that sound it does as it throws the shingle up the beach. Do you know the poem *Dover Beach*, Leonard? It's by Matthew Arnold. He's not much read now, I don't think, but the poem is a favourite of mine, ever since I was a boy. I think I must have learned it at school. We used to have to learn poetry off by heart in those days. *Dover Beach* has these lines I've never forgotten and they came to me this morning when I was standing alone by the sea, feeling so sorry for myself.

Listen! You hear the grating roar
Of pebbles which the waves draw back, and fling,

139

At their return, up the high strand,
Begin, and cease, and then again begin,
With tremulous cadence slow, and bring
The eternal note of sadness in.

And then the first glimmer of day edged over the horizon, picking up the whiteness of the foam that crested the waves as they crashed up the beach. Those lines were so vivid to me at that moment. It was if they were part of me, part of the sea, the beach – a kind of transcending moment. Matthew Arnold was talking about the loss of faith, something he felt very strongly about. But as the lines kept rolling and rolling around my head I began to see the whole thing differently. The noise of the sea clawing its way up the beach, forever scouring away at the sand and the shingle, seemed to be scrubbing away at me, delving deep into my soul and trying to wash me clean, to make me pure again. It was to do with taking me back to a time when we were not weighed down as we are now, when life was simpler and more instinctive, when your deeds did not always carry consequences.

My thoughts went back to a time when like today I was standing on a beach, looking out to sea. But it was warm day and I must have been about seven years old, one of hundreds of kids enjoying a day at the beach. I think it was a church outing or something and for once my father was with us. He rarely came with us on day trips in the holidays because he was always working. We made sand castles together and he showed me how damp sand made the best castles, and how to tap the bucket before turning out the sand. We built a moat around our castle and I carried bucket after bucket of water up from the sea to fill the moat but most of it just soaked away. So we waited for the tide to come up the beach to where our castle stood with its stiff flags made from cigarette packets covering the battlements. The sea flowed first into the moat, quickly filling it and then began eroding the towers and gatehouses that we had so meticulously constructed. I didn't mind seeing all our work destroyed because it was something that me and my dad had made together, and that was a rare thing.

The day was coming to an end and we knew that we would have to make tracks back to the bus but I wanted one last go in the sea before we departed. My father rolled up his trouser bottoms and we paddled in the sea together and then he took my hand in his and we just stood there gazing out to sea, enjoying the last of the day. My father rarely touched me, never gave me a hug or patted my head. He just wasn't made that way. I'd see dads grabbing their sons when they'd won a race at the school sports or scored a goal or hit a six but my dad would never do things like that. But on that summer's day as he and I stood in the sea, the water cool upon our legs and the sun tingling on my puny shoulders, he held my hand and said: 'It doesn't get much better than this, does it, son?' And then, so as not to get my feet covered in sand again, he took me on his shoulders and carried me back up the beach, where my mother was packing all the paraphernalia that we'd brought with us. My dad wrapped me in a towel and helped me change back into my clothes and then sat me in a deckchair while he dried my feet and carefully put on the white socks that I never wore at any other time of the year except at the beach and buckled up my new brown sandals with their stiff straps.

I remembered that day this morning as I stood on that cold beach, feeling so low, waiting for the dawn to come up. That was the first and last time that I came so close to my father. He revealed something about himself that day that thereafter was always kept locked

141

away, and when I was old enough to find the key to unlock the emotions that still lurked within him I chose not to. I chose to be the best in school, to put even more distance between us, to make him feel even worse about himself. I didn't do this out of malice because in one way I wanted him to be proud of me but we were living in different worlds by then and we didn't share a common tongue any more.

And now I look at myself and ask the obvious question: Have I become my father? Was I always destined to be like him? Is it some kind of genetic predisposition to tread the path I seem to have stumbled down? I need to find a way out of the mess I'm in but I don't know how. I need a light and a compass, Leonard, and I can't find either.

CHAPTER 14

Molly seemed to take Harry's tardy return with a pinch of salt, with no raised eyebrows or a knowing look that said *I don't believe you*. In fact, she was quite solicitous about the tribulations he had endured with the car. But she still got in a little dig.

'I told you I thought your exhaust was sounding a bit throaty. You should have had the car serviced before you went. But anyway, never mind, you're home now.'

As she stood in the kitchen, pouring Harry a cup of tea, he tried to gauge whether she had changed while he was away. Had she found the space she was looking for, had she furnished it with new ideas, new ways of living, had she perhaps populated it with someone else, someone with whom she could live without the need for long, meaningful chats in the attic and emails that weighed you in the balance and found you woefully wanting? No, there could be no one else. After all, he'd only been away for five days. But now that he looked at her more closely as she moved around the kitchen while he drank his tea, there was something different about her, something almost imperceptibly different, but there all the same.

'Have you done anything different with your hair while I was away?'

'It's a little shorter and I've gone a couple of shades lighter.'

Molly was standing with her back to Harry as she wiped the worktop. She paused, cloth in hand and stood motionless. The kitchen breathed in and waited to exhale, the flowers stood stock-still in the vase on the windowsill and even the ticking of the clock became muted.

'It suits you,' he said after what seemed like an age.

'Thank you, Harry. By the way, I've changed my hours at work. I've re-arranged everything to have a day off tomorrow and every week.'

'But I work on a Monday. We arranged our hours to more-or-less coincide. You said you wanted us to spend more free time together.'

'Well, that was then and this is now. Anyway, you spend this precious free time mostly on your own, either on the computer compiling a quiz, tracing our ancestors or endlessly watching News 24 on the television or, worse, repeats of *Only Fools And Houses*. You must know the scripts off by heart by now. If I suggest we go somewhere for a drive or a pub lunch, you pull a face as long as a fiddle. So I thought I'd find a day for myself. Tomorrow I'm having a spa day with Angela.'

'A spa day?'

'Yes, Harry. You've heard of them. I expect you've forgotten but Christopher and Hazel bought me vouchers for my last birthday. You must remember; you bought me that slow-cooker. You were going through your economy drive phase. It's still in the box. Oh yes, I meant to tell you. I've re-joined the gym and I've managed to work in a time slot every day. It's all on the calendar.'

Harry had a quick sandwich for lunch and then set about emptying the car, while Molly went to spend some time with her father, who Harry was relieved to know was still in good health. Why were women so difficult to comprehend? They go to such lengths to establish a routine that suits them and supposedly benefits their husband. *Harry, we must ensure that we build in enough time together when we retire. I've read that retirement can be a death knell for relationships*

144

because couples take each other for granted and do their own thing. The next thing you know they're in the divorce court. And now it's all change and they need time on their own. And what about going to the gym every day? What had sparked this desire to keep fit? Molly had always kept herself pretty trim. She still had quite a good figure really. Admittedly her bosoms sagged a bit these days and her backside was a bit more prominent but women tend to let themselves go in middle age, don't they?

He was pondering the mysteries of womankind as he carried in the umpteenth box of wine, ready to be catalogued into his 'cellar' when the house phone rang. Irritated at being interrupted, he snatched at the receiver brusquely. The west country burr of the speaker brought Harry quickly down to earth.

'Harry, is that you? Good journey back?'

'Why are you ringing me at home? My wife could have picked up the phone.'

'I need to ask you a few more questions and I've got some interesting news for you.'

Harry listened as DS Wilkins told him that the French police had checked all the garages in the Guingamp area and no Volvo car belonging to someone answering Alex's description had been repaired that week.

'But she telephoned the garage on her mobile when she was in the car with me. They were going to deliver the car to the cottage.'

'She was obviously making it up to keep you believing the breakdown story. You said yourself that you didn't actually see her off. Her actual departure from the cottage is even more interesting because we have a witness. I gather you have a French neighbour called Guillaume'

Wilkins explained that the French police had called on Guillaume as a matter of routine and discovered that on the morning that Alex left he was up early checking his traps for coypu, an interloper that had no place in the rivers and streams of Brittany and one that he was single-handedly trying to eradicate. It was around 7am and still quite dark. Guillaume was on his way back to his house when he was taken short near Harry's cottage. He was taking a leak on the drive when the headlights of a car swept down the lane. Guillaume was curious as the lane was residents only and he wanted to know who was taking a short cut that early in the morning. So he hid behind the hedge to catch whoever it was driving past. But as the car approached the bend outside the cottage it cut its engine and lights, and glided to a stop so close to Guillaume that he had to retreat further into the undergrowth to avoid being seen. Guillaume tried to get a sight of the driver but it was too dark. What happened next surprised Guillaume because who should appear out of the cottage but a woman carrying a suitcase. She quickly got into the car which immediately drove off, its headlights only coming on when it reached the bridge.

'Your neighbour was really shocked, Harry, because as he told the froggy police: "The woman was not Harry's wife. She was much younger and blonde. And anyway Molly was not with Harry. He told us he was on his own."'

Harry could sense that Wilkins was enjoying this latest twist in the tale, Guillaume of all people seeing a woman leaving the cottage in the early hours. No wonder he and Sylvie were so cool towards him on that last day. Harry knew that he was never going to keep this story from Molly. This surely couldn't get any worse.

'And there's more, Harry. There's more. It seems that this Guillaume chap likes to keep an eye on the comings and goings of your visitors. Bit of a nosey parker, as it were, or perhaps he needs to get a life, because he clocks all the cars that are parked on your drive. He says that the mysterious car that didn't want to be seen had been there before. He's pretty sure that it was parked on your property for a week in October. Now what do you think of that? Are you still there, Harry?'

Harry was having trouble taking all this in.

'What are you saying? That Alex, or someone who knew Alex, had been to the cottage before? That doesn't make sense.'

'Nothing makes sense in this case, Harry. Mysterious women, mysterious cars – it's like something out of a thriller. Which leads me to the obvious question, Harry. Do you keep a record of your guests – names, addresses and the like?'

Of course! There would be a record of who booked in October. Molly organised the bookings and kept a list of the weeks allocated to visitors to make sure there were no double bookings. He found the diary that Molly used exclusively for the cottage. As he flipped through the pages, he remembered that October bookings were uncommon because if you were looking for a bit of warmth you were unlikely to find it in Brittany at that time of the year. He flipped through the pages: August... September... October. First week nothing, second week the same, no, there was a booking in the name of Richardson for two people and then he recalled that it was a very late enquiry, which Molly was reluctant to take because guests were likely to use more heat in the cottage than the payment was worth. But the woman had been quite persuasive and said that

147

she and her husband needed a break because they were just getting over a family bereavement. Molly was of course won over by that and took the booking.

Harry gave the details to Detective Sergeant Wilkins who said that he'd put money on it that the details would all be false. But they had to check every lead.

'And Harry, I know I shouldn't give you advice about how to deal with your better half but I think the time has come when you're going to have to come clean with your missus because otherwise the whole thing's gonna get messier and messier. You get my drift?'

Harry decides to finish unpacking the car later. He needs a sit down and a cup of coffee. He is just filling the kettle when the phone rings again. He thinks *not Wilkins again!* But it's Molly's mobile that is ringing. She's left it on the work surface, charging. The voice is male. It's someone wanting Molly. Won't leave a name – says he'll call back later and rings off abruptly. When Harry puts the phone down, the man's voice still resonates. It's a younger man's voice and he clearly did not expect Harry to pick up. He checks Molly's received calls in the hope that it will say unknown number but the name Paul illuminates the screen.

~

Later that day Harry and Molly are seated around the kitchen table, their knives and forks pecking at the cottage pie that Molly has prepared.

'By the way, you had a call earlier from some chap. Didn't leave any details. You forgot to take your mobile with you.'

Molly gets up rather quickly, the chair scraping on the tiled floor, and goes to her phone, which is still charging on the work surface. She flicks it open and checks the call.

'No number. No doubt someone selling something.'

Dear Leonard,

This Alex business is getting out of hand. I just can't fathom it. I've got pieces of a strange jigsaw floating around in my head and I can't fit them together to make a coherent whole. One piece has Alex standing pathetically in the supermarket car park on that blustery day last week, a seemingly random encounter that ends up with her staying at the cottage. Another has Alex, or someone connected with her, staying at the cottage some three weeks before, presumably under an assumed name. How does this fit together? Did Alex pre-plan that meeting at LeClerc in order to get back into the cottage and, if so, why? But to meet up with me, Alex must have been following me, waiting for an opportunity for me to park somewhere and then contrive a chance encounter. Surely not. After all, I have free will, don't I? I could have said no and merely dropped her at the tourist office. But then I remember her eyes, those imploring eyes, and her body huddled against the wind like an orphan of the storm. Could I have been so taken in that I dropped my guard from the sensible, logical being that would normally never have offered an attractive stranger a bed for the night? But that could be the only explanation and what's more Alex contrived a further night in the cottage. Am I that gullible, Leonard; so easily duped?

So, all that talking on the first night, asking me about myself, finding out about my love of art, my passion for Vincent's paintings – that was all part of the game, to keep me sweet and to make sure that she could continue to manipulate me. She had me dangling on her line all the time. She wasn't really interested in me at all. And Molly's name! She let slip Molly's name on that first night, which surprised me, but she quickly glossed over it. She must have dealt with Molly to book the cottage in October and probably spoke to her on the phone. I can't believe people can be so devious.

The pieces of the jigsaw are coming together now. Alex and an accomplice had booked the cottage probably as a base for their operations, maybe to gather together the goods they were planning to smuggle into Britain. No doubt these books and maps were coming from different sources. So why didn't they just pack up the car and bring them over by ferry when they had the opportunity? Something must have prevented them. Wilkins said the police had had their eye on the Plymouth dealer for some time, so perhaps Alex got wind that the authorities were on to them. Maybe they decided to lie low until the coast was clear. So why did they need to get back into the cottage?

But there's even more on my plate, isn't there? Who the hell is this Paul phoning Molly and she making out it's nothing. I thought that things were getting back to normal between Molly and me. No, perhaps I'm reading too much into this and there's a perfectly reasonable explanation. This business in France has left me shattered and I'm viewing everything and everyone with suspicion. I mean Molly is the last person I know who would be unfaithful.

I wish I had your knowledge and experience of the opposite sex. Of course I realise that, in spite of the creative inspiration they have given you in your work, your entanglements with women may have come at a personal cost. But I guess you wouldn't have wanted it any other way. And at least you've lived life to the full. I envy you, Leonard, but I've never wanted to be you. I suppose you're the alter ego that I can safely switch on whenever I want.

Oh my God! I just said that Molly was the last person I know who would be unfaithful and she would say the same of me!

CHAPTER 15

Harry's at the gallery next day, his first day back since returning from France. He arrives to find a note in his pigeonhole. HR wants to see him straightaway. Harry is not enamoured of *Personnel* as he still likes to call it but he foregoes the cup of coffee he looks forward to before starting his shift to go immediately upstairs.

'Sit down, Harry. How was the trip to France?' asks Tim, Head of HR, not really wishing for an answer. 'I'll cut to the chase. We've had a complaint about you. Received it while you were away. Thought we'd better deal with it as soon as you got back. Here's a copy of the letter we got last week. Take your time reading it. I'll be back in five.'

The door closes and Harry is left alone. The letter has an address in Cheltenham and the writer is a woman. Harry notices that the font is Comic Sans and sniffs loudly.

I would like to complain in the strongest possible terms about the treatment I received yesterday from one of your assistants. I was in the gallery with my daughter, looking at the Augustus John portrait of Dylan Thomas when I was accosted by Harry Dymond (according to his name tag). I was telling my daughter a little of the life of Dylan Thomas when Mr Dymond interrupted me and told me that what I was saying was incorrect. He then proceeded to put me 'right'. When I informed him that I did not need his 'help', he told me in no uncertain terms that it was important that children were always told the truth, as if I needed any advice on how to bring up my own child.

I found Mr Dymond's manner entirely inappropriate. He was rude and overbearing, and certainly his behaviour was not what one would expect in what purports to be the national museum of Wales. Mr Dymond's attitude would certainly not encourage me to visit the museum in the future.

Harry puts down the letter as Tim returns.

'I've already telephoned Mrs Wainwright and naturally apologised to her if her visit to the museum had been marred in any way. That was the least I could do in the circumstances. I wasn't prejudging the outcome of this meeting by the way and I told her that obviously I would have to listen to your version of events when you returned from holiday but as a disappointed customer she deserved an apology. So, Harry, what would you like to say about all this?'

Harry composes himself before answering. He stares down at Tim's desk and can see Tim's fingers lightly drumming on a lined writing pad whose blankness awaits the pencil gripped in the poised fingers of his other hand. The desk is otherwise bare apart from a photograph, which is at an angle for every visitor to see, of two children - a boy and a girl in school uniform - each with a smug and toothy grin, as if they are enjoying Harry's discomfort.

Harry recalls the encounter he had had with Mrs Wainwright. He'd been left feeling a bit rebuffed but he was only trying to be helpful and, yes, informative. The letter describes him as rude and that shocks him. He never intended to be rude. He looks at Tim whose eyebrows are arching in anticipation of Harry's explanation.

'She's right about the portrait of Dylan Thomas. I was standing nearby and she was talking very loudly about him to her daughter, who frankly looked bored to death. I'd seen them traipsing through the gallery all morning with Mrs Wainwright pontificating to her daughter whenever they stopped at a particular painting. She was saying that Dylan Thomas drank himself to death, that he was on a binge, drinking whisky after whisky and had died of alcohol poisoning. Well, that's the conventional wisdom on the subject, isn't it? And I wasn't going to say that she was wrong but I merely said that there was a theory that, while it was true that he'd consumed huge amounts of alcohol, his actual death was caused by a private doctor who injected him with morphine, which sent him into a coma from which he never recovered. That was all I said but she seemed to take umbrage at this and started raising her voice at me. I did say something about children needing all the facts but she hit the roof at that point. I wasn't trying to say that she was a bad mother or anything like that. Anyway, she stormed off then, dragging the poor child with her. I should have reported it, I suppose, but I didn't expect that she would make an official complaint. I can assure you that I was not rude or overbearing.'

Tim has been taking copious notes of Harry's version of events. In fact Harry marvels at how quickly he has filled the page in a long hand that, even upside down, looks flawless.

'Look, Harry, you've settled in well here. You work hard, you're flexible about your hours, filling in at short notice and you know your stuff when it comes to art, not that it's a requirement of the job, but you still do it well. But – and you may not like what I have to say – you can come across as a bit soulless at times when you're dealing with the public. Ask you for information and you're on the ball. But did you really feel the need to give a customer the very latest theory on the death of Wales's greatest poet and make them feel small in front of their child? Dylan Thomas was an alcoholic and

154

what she was telling her daughter was essentially true, if perhaps not clinically correct.'

Harry wants to say something, anything, but even he sees that Tim is in mid flow and won't be interrupted. Harry clenches his buttocks like a small boy waiting for the cane outside the Head's office. The toothy twosome are really enjoying this and Harry has to avert their gaze.

'Look, I'm not going to make this a disciplinary matter although there are grounds for me to do just that. If I thought you had been deliberately rude, Harry, you'd get a warning and your days here would be numbered. But being rude and appearing to be rude look the same to the person at the receiving end. Do you understand what I'm getting at? Harry, try to cultivate a little more empathy. The public, our customers, come in here for lots of reasons: for study, for inspiration, to be virtuous culture-seekers and sometimes just to get out of the rain. Be there if they want help, directions, whatever, but don't talk down to them. Mrs Wainwright's letter is over the top but you gave her cause. Anyway, off you go and don't feel so bad about this. Just learn from the experience, okay?'

Harry does not feel he has the strength to rise but he slowly gets to his feet. He thanks Tim out of courtesy and makes for the door.

'Oh, I nearly forgot. There's a personal letter here for you, which came yesterday. Maybe you've forgotten but staff are not allowed to receive correspondence at the museum's address. Anyway, you'd better start your shift. The doors are opening soon.'

Harry stuffs the letter into his pocket, not giving it much of a thought. He knows that he is over-reacting but Mrs Wainwright's letter has touched him deeply.

155

How is it that everything he seems to do these days is misunderstood, his motives misinterpreted?

The day grinds very slowly and he finds it difficult to feel enthusiastic. When asked for information by visitors he feels threatened. What if I say the wrong thing? He can't wait for his shift to end.

The platform at Queen Street Station is crowded with pre-Christmas shoppers and office workers. Harry just wants the sanctuary of the railway carriage and hopefully a seat on his own where he can collect his thoughts. He sits next to a window that is steamed up but he feels no need to see the city centre as the train rumbles its way into the suburbs. He suddenly remembers the letter in his pocket. Who could be writing to him at the museum? He rips it open and takes out a single sheet of paper on which a short message is typed. It reads:

Harry, I'm sorry it all went wrong. I need to see you. Can you meet me this Friday in Bristol outside Temple Meads Station at midday? Please don't tell the police. I have to trust you.

Alex

Harry's train arrived late at Bristol Temple Meads and it was past noon when he emerged from the station, but there was no Alex to meet him. He looked around the confines of Brunel's edifice and on a normal day he might have paused to admire this monument to the golden age of steam but this was far from normal. He had re-arranged his shift at the museum, which he had done reluctantly, not wishing to cause any waves after the issue of the complaint but when he'd said he had to take his wife for an *important* hospital appointment no one in the museum office wanted to ask any more questions.

Of course, what occupied his mind now was the sheer madness of being here, meeting someone who was being pursued by the police. *So, Harry,* Wilkins would say, *you still maintain your complete innocence in this whole affair. You were an unwitting pawn, duped by a scheming woman who used her feminine charms to seduce you into acting as a mule. Of course, we accept your version of events. But how do you explain meeting this self-same woman in Bristol? Just bumped into her at the zoo, did you?*

Harry looked anxiously at his watch. It was 12.15. Alex wasn't coming. He'd been made to look a fool again. He was about to turn back into the station when a green Volvo came to a halt in front of him. The passenger door was clumsily thrown open from inside and Alex beckoned him to get in. He had hardly got his seat belt on when the car exited the station approach and sped off along Temple Gate through the busy lunchtime traffic.

'I see the car's back on the road,' he sneered. 'Marvellous mechanics, the French.'

Alex did not reply but continued to head uphill, taking Harry via a circuitous route that even included Clifton Suspension Bridge. Harry wondered if this was a tour entitled 'Isambard Kingdom Brunel: Landmarks of Bristol.' The car finally halted outside a Georgian house in Clifton Village. Alex gestured for Harry to get out and he followed her into a ground floor flat. After shutting and locking the door, Alex went to the large living room window and looked out before re-arranging the net curtain to cover the frame.

'I'm sorry for all this skulduggery and for keeping you waiting at the station but I needed to be sure no one was following you. I took a risk picking you up at the station but it seemed the best way for us to meet.'

'*You* took a risk. I'm risking everything meeting you. You set me up; you played me for a fool. I could be on remand at this moment awaiting trial on a charge of handling stolen goods. I could have informed the police.'

Alex stood motionless in front of the window and for the first time since being reunited with Harry she met his gaze. Her hair was scraped back and pinned carelessly; she was wearing no make-up and she was breathing irregularly.

'I know you could and I wouldn't blame you if you had but I needed to speak with you and...' her lip trembled slightly... 'I'm glad you came. I really am.'

She made coffee in the corner kitchen while Harry sat in front of an ancient gas fire whose elements were blackened with soot. He hadn't paid much attention to his surroundings before now but a glance revealed a threadbare carpet, grubby paintwork and a single bed that doubled as a sofa, its cushions haphazardly scattered over a striped throw.

'I'm sorry but there aren't any biscuits,' Alex called from the kitchen, as if she was having a girl friend rounded for elevenses. 'I'm only using this place for today and I don't know where everything is.'

When they were seated, with Harry remaining obdurately silent, Alex finally said that she wanted to come clean about everything and what she was going to say was the truth.

She *was* an antiques dealer but in Witney, not Shepton Mallet. It had been her second husband's business and as far as she was concerned the shop was doing well. They were very much part of the green welly crowd, lots of social functions, the whole shooting match. But when her husband suddenly died, she found the business was mortgaged up to the hilt and had debts on all sides. He had been living a completely Walter Mitty life and had left her to pick up the pieces. She managed to stave off the collapse of the business by soft-talking the bank and re-mortgaging the family home to inject some cash into the shop. She also used her initiative to develop links with suppliers in Normandy and change the business's image from dusty carriage clocks and stuffed birds to French shabby chic. She would make regular trips from Portsmouth, leaving her husband's daughter, Emily, in charge of the shop. But then the credit crunch hit and the vultures started to gather again. She had worked so hard and all her efforts seemed doomed to failure. The house was repossessed and she and Emily were forced to live in a small flat above the shop. The one good thing to emerge from the crisis was the bond she forged with Emily. They were determined not to go under in spite of the misfortunes swirling around them.

159

It was on a trip to Caen to source supplies that she met up with a dealer – she called him Jean-Luc - who offered her a way out. He traded in antiquarian books and maps and, if she was interested, he could cut her in. He was looking for someone who could take the odd parcel across the Channel and the rewards were high, provided she didn't enquire into the provenance of the goods in question. She refused point blank, realising that this trade was obviously illegal. But when she returned from that particular trip, she found that one of her creditors had given her 14 days' notice to cough up or the bailiffs would be paying a visit. Having lost the house, she now faced the loss of the business and the flat she shared with Emily.

'So I decided that I would put my morals aside and make a few trips with these 'goods'. But it was going to be finite, a few trips just to get some cash together and keep my head above water.'

'But you knew it was illegal, didn't you?'

'Of course I did, and even now I can't believe I did it. I wasn't brought up to do things like that. But I was desperate to save the business, which had become *my* business and I couldn't bear to see it collapse. So, I admit, I blanked out all the circumstances that would make a person reject doing such a thing. I reduced the whole operation to a parcel, whose contents I never saw, being delivered to someone I didn't know and I convinced myself that no one was getting hurt or losing money. These were books and maps that were lying on dusty shelves somewhere in Europe, uncared for probably and often unseen for years, quietly decaying. In my head I reduced it to someone buying a hooky DVD at a car boot sale or in the back of a pub. Someone says it's off the back of the lorry and you say

160

okay, nudge nudge, no questions asked. What you don't see can't harm you. We've all done it.'

'But these 'hooky' parcels contained rare volumes of great antiquity and value, and did you not know that often the maps would be torn out of books with razor blades? The heritage of centuries ripped apart just for a quick buck.'

'Thank you, Harry, that makes me feel much better. Of course, I knew this! But it was in some other part of my mind. I knew it was wrong but I got hooked. The money was saving my business and it was easy money. In all the trips I made I had no problems. The customs people would stop and search the car from time to time but they got to know me and eventually they would wave me through. No one suspected me.'

'So how did I get involved? You said your trips were to Normandy, not Brittany.'

'I was coming to that. One of the English dealers got greedy and careless. The idea was to drip-feed these maps and books into the hands of private dealers but he flooded the market with too much stuff in too short a time. He was picked up by the police and, although he didn't inform on Jean-Luc or me, we realised that Normandy was getting too hot so we switched to Brittany. But by this time, I'd decided that I was going to get out. It was too risky and…'

'…and you'd made enough money out of it by then.'

'I was going to say that I'd come to realise that, in spite of what I wanted to believe, I was just a common criminal. Believe me, Harry. This was organised crime and I was no better than a drug dealer or a bank robber. I was determined to finish with it.'

'So why didn't you?'

'I tried but …we decided to use the Plymouth-Roscoff route and Jean-Luc had lined up this dealer in

161

Plymouth. We did one run and it worked out OK. I told Jean-Luc that I wanted out but he got awkward. He threatened me and worse he said that he would harm my stepdaughter if I didn't do one last run. He said he was waiting for a supply of goods to come up from the south of France but it was slower than usual because the French police were getting wise to the operation. The goods had been split into smaller parcels to make it easier to avoid detection but they were going to arrive in dribs and drabs. We needed a safe house to store the goods as they came up from the south. I hit on the idea of renting a cottage close to the N12 but secluded enough to mask any comings and goings. I looked in the Chez Nous brochure and your cottage was just perfect. I imagine you wrote the description. I looked at what your ad was saying. I can remember some of your phrases now...*pretty, secluded cottage in a wooded dell...ideal for exploring the delights of the Côtes D'Armor...'*

'And you thought...*pretty secluded cottage ...perfect for hiding away literary and geographical artefacts stolen to order.'*

'It wasn't like that! I was trapped and I just wanted to get this over with.'

'So what went wrong?'

'Everything. Only half the expected goods turned up because the police were closing in. We were getting jumpy and were expecting to get raided at every moment. Your neighbour didn't help. We kept seeing him prowling around. On a couple of occasions, I saw him looking up at the bedroom window when I was changing. I think he was just nosey or pervy but we were getting scared. In the end we decided to leave what we had in the loft. We reckoned nobody would go up there. It was full of droppings and the odd dead mouse. We got duplicate keys cut and planned to come back when the coast was clear. We met your caretaker and he said we were the last guests of the season, so we thought we just had to turn up, collect the goods and go.'

'And when you came back you found the cottage occupied…by me.'

'Exactly. We hadn't bargained on anyone being there. We assumed you were the owner because you were on your own and on that first day we drove past in a van and you were talking to your neighbour as if you knew each other, so we put two and two together.'

'So why didn't you just wait until I'd gone out, get your stuff and scarper? I'd be none the wiser and I wouldn't have got arrested by the police'

'We learned from another contact that the police on both sides of the Channel were on full alert. They would be expecting a delivery and there was a chance that my cover was blown. We both agreed that this would be the last operation. It was getting too hot and I think even Jean-Luc was getting cold feet by this time anyway. But how were we to get the last parcel to England? Then Jean-Luc hit on the idea of getting you to bring over the parcel. I was against it, Harry! But there seemed no other way, so we came up with the idea of the broken down car and I would meet up with you accidentally on purpose and give you a sob story about needing a place to stay. I didn't think you'd fall for it but you did.'

'Yes, I was a complete chump, wasn't I?'

'Not a chump, Harry, but a very kind man. I can't say how sorry I am that I used you in this way. But I honestly thought that all you had to do was deliver the parcel. Neither of us knew that the police were keeping tabs on the Plymouth dealer. We didn't know how close they all were in finding us and they still might. I had to drive all the way up to Boulogne and cross via the Channel Tunnel, because they were watching all the ferry ports.'

'My heart bleeds for you.'

'I don't blame you for how you feel. You have every right to hate me. But I could have lain low after all this business. The authorities don't seem to have got anything on me and there's a chance they won't link me with anything. You could of course go straight to the police but obviously I don't want you to. But I hope you see that I was prepared to risk everything by meeting you today. I can't make amends for what has happened but I wanted to say that I am sorry for what I did and I mean that. If I'm arrested by the police, I'll tell them the truth about your role in all this, I promise you. I'll them that you acted in all innocence.'

'Does your stepdaughter know all about this? Was she part of the operation?'

'She didn't know at first but she got suspicious when the business seemed to be improving rather quickly while sales remained flat. She's not daft. That's another reason why I decided to give it all up. This is her friend's flat, by the way. She's a student here and it seemed as good a place as any to meet up with you. We'll need to leave shortly by the way because she's due back in an hour. So can we at least depart as friends? Harry, I want you know that when you made that advance to me, you know, outside the bedroom, I wanted it to go further. And I know this sounds perverse but in rejecting you I probably did the only decent thing I've done to you. I said no because you deserved better than a cheap fuck with someone like me. Your wife is lucky to have you because you're a rare commodity these days – you're a decent man.'

Listening to Alex, Harry had wanted to vent all the feelings that were strangling him inside but at this final remark everything sank to the pit of his stomach and drained him of emotion.

'By the way, are you going to tell me your real name? I'm guessing it's not Alex.'

'I'm Alex to you and that should be enough. Names are just labels. So Harry, what do you intend to do when you go back to Cardiff. Turn me in?'

'Look, Alex, even if you've finally told me the truth today, the fact that can't be swept under the carpet is that you used me – the Good Samaritan, was it? – as part of your criminal activities. You put me at risk and by doing that you risked the well being of my family with all the repercussions. I can't say what I'm going to do if the police come calling again. I don't choose to be the one who brings you down, if that should happen. At the moment the police seem to accept that I was just an innocent bit player in this enterprise. But if I am dragged into this, I will protect myself because in doing that I protect my family. So I'm not going to turn you in as you say, but I'm not going to lie for you.'

'Thank you, Harry. That's all I can ask.'

'There's one last thing I'd like to know, Alex. This meeting has been all about you and me but the one person who seems strangely absent from our thoughts is this Jean-Luc. We're skulking about trying to keep our heads down but where is he in all this and what is he doing?'

'I can't tell you that because I don't know. We crossed the Channel together but then went our separate ways. I don't know if he's still in the country or back in France. I don't know anything about his background or where he lived. He would phone me and we would meet up. He knows everything about me but he was and still is a bit of a mystery to me. We agreed never to see each other again but I'm still looking over my shoulder and feel his presence everywhere.'

'Seems like I wasn't the only one to be taken in.'

Alex offered to take Harry back to the station. He would have preferred to bring it to an end there, to walk away with that phrase ringing in his mind – 'you're a decent man.' It somehow gave the whole episode with Alex a dramatic finality. But as it was he didn't know how to get back to Temple Meads so he agreed to a lift. He left the flat first, with Alex carefully closing the front door behind her and then posting the keys through the letterbox.

There was a small park in front of the house with a group of young mothers pushing buggies in which swathed babies slept contentedly. They were too preoccupied with their chatter to notice the man taking photos of the autumn foliage and certainly did not see him turn and point his camera with its long lens at Harry and Alex as they proceeded to walk down the steps (click), get into her car (click) and drive off (click, click).

Harry got back to Cardiff in time to coincide with his normal daily routine. He entered the kitchen to find Molly peeling carrots. She filled the kettle while he flicked through the post, but there was nothing worth opening. Although this was a perfectly normal domestic homecoming – *Good day at the gallery, dear? Yes, and you? Fine* – he felt obliged to concoct some tale of his spurious working day to confirm its normality. He was going to relate some mundane incident when Molly turned towards the cupboard to get out two cups and he noticed her face. She was flushed, but not just with the flush of exertion, no, it was more like a glow, the skin of her face seemed tauter, her eyes brighter, she had a

166

bloom that he hadn't seen since they were young together. It surprised him.

'Harry, what are you staring at?'

'Nothing,' he said. 'What's for tea?'

Dear Leonard,

I know it was crazy to meet with Alex. If Wilkins found out, I'd now be sitting in a police cell in Plymouth prior to being remanded in custody. I went to Bristol full of anger and I wanted to get my own back on Alex but in the end I didn't say what I wanted to say because she seemed to be genuinely ashamed about getting me involved in this business. Of course, I can't be sure. I don't read women very well but the cool, sophisticated woman I met in Brittany seemed to have disappeared. Frankly she looked in a right old state. She's scared – scared of being caught by the police, of course – but she's scared of this Jean-Luc, too. He's a nasty bit of work. For my part, I just want to keep all this from Molly. I just want to get back to normality.

But Molly is becoming more of a worry. Since I got back from France, I've noticed that Molly is different, in all sorts of ways. Before I left, she was giving me the third degree every day about all my faults but that has stopped. I'm not saying I want her to resume the onslaught on the foibles of my character but, nevertheless, it's a very abrupt cessation of hostilities. I wouldn't say that she's cool towards me but she's very matter of fact about everything. It's a bit unnerving I can tell you. Another difference is her appearance. She's looking trim, very trim; she told me that she'd lost a bit of weight and said going to the gym regularly was helping. But it's not just her figure that has changed; it's her face, too. She looks different, more pinky and shiny, like the women in her magazines who use this rejuvenating cream or some such. But I know that women in magazines get touched up, their photos I mean. Molly is real.

And the other difference is her demeanour. She's forever trilling around the house, singing snatches of songs and is very full of beans. I find this very disconcerting, Leonard, especially in light of that call from that man called Paul. What do you think it could mean? I'm afraid to ask because I fear the worst and I don't want to bring up the subject with her because I've got my own secrets.

There's worse. I nearly forgot. My friend Mike told me that he was down the Bay at the weekend. There was some sort of continental food fair going on in the Oval Basin. He took a stroll over to the Norwegian Church where they've got a café and who should he see but Molly. But she wasn't alone; she was with a man, a much younger man. Now Mike's a good chap but a bit slow on the uptake. He didn't see anything odd in all this thankfully but my head's in a spin I can tell you. The thing is, if Molly was having an affair – I can't believe I'm saying the word – why would she be seeing this bloke down the Bay of all places. You're not supposed to do it in your own back yard, are you? So, I don't know what to think.

And there's something else. I promised myself that I wouldn't tell you this but I can't stop myself. I opened Molly's underwear drawer yesterday. Now before you get any wrong ideas, I'm not into anything like that. You see I always keep some euros in the house, just to tide us over if we go to France. I keep them in an envelope in Molly's drawer, just in case we get burgled. Burglars are not going to look for money in a knicker drawer, are they? Molly says even pervy burglars are not going to rummage through any of her knickers because they'd hardly arouse anyone. But that's not the point. Having come back from France, I was putting some euros back in the drawer and, well, I don't know what to say, but Molly had new knickers in there but not her usual fit-for-purpose ones. These were, well, all

169

lacy and shiny and there were bras to match as well. It was underwear more suited to a …a younger woman, to a woman who wants someone to see her in her underwear, not like Molly who's quite coy about that sort of thing. So, seeing that underwear and actually holding it in my hands has made me feel very confused, I can tell you.

I think we're both thinking the same thing, aren't we? What am I going to do, Leonard? What on earth am I going to do?

CHAPTER 17

When Harry next turned up for work, he was met by one of the assistant secretaries who quietly put a letter in his hand, saying that she'd intercepted it so as not to get him into trouble. This was becoming a problem. Surely Alex was not continuing to write to him? He found a quiet corner and opened the envelope. Its contents shocked him and for a second he thought he might pass out. There were three photos of him leaving the Bristol flat with Alex. The clarity was incredible and one in particular of them walking down the steps of the house to the pavement suggested an intimacy that belied the truth. His immediate thought was that he had been shadowed by the police and this was the evidence they were looking for, evidence that connected him with Alex and would surely result in his conviction. Had they picked her up by now? He almost failed to see the note inside the envelope. He opened it out and tried to focus on the words:

Just in case you get any ideas of shopping Alex, these photos might just end up in the wrong hands!

The rest of the day went badly. The assistants had to attend a refresher session on manual handling before the museum opened at 10.00am. Harry found it difficult to concentrate and he thought he'd heard it all before. The trainer was a woman of considerable bulk who could kick sand in the face of a Russian weightlifter. She would have no trouble manually handling a Sherman tank, he thought. She droned on for about half an hour and Harry just drifted off. He was being propelled forward by events over which he no longer had any control. He just couldn't fathom the photos. Who had taken them? Did Alex know they were being taken? Did she arrange it all as a sort of insurance policy? Was the meeting in Bristol just another farce to make him look a fool? And then there was the mysterious Jean-Luc. What part was he still playing in this affair?

The trainer jolted Harry out of his torpor by asking him to demonstrate lifting a heavy object. He got it all wrong and a few titters erupted from the back of the room. The trainer remarked sarcastically that if he did that during the course of his work they would be manually handling him to A & E. More titters. Harry flushed from head to toe and cast a long glance at a bodily frame that would not be out of place in a Welsh front row. Harry saw the words coming a mile off but could not intercept them before they left his mouth. He said: 'At least I wouldn't need a flatbed truck to get to hospital.'

When the session ended, Harry approached the trainer, knowing what he had to do. But she wouldn't allow him to speak, gathered up her stuff and stormed out. Harry knew in whose direction she would be headed. He spent a miserable day. The museum was staging another dinosaur exhibition and was full of school parties, with children scurrying everywhere with clipboards and pencils, while harassed teachers shepherded them around the exhibits like anxious collies.

During his breaks, none of the other assistants seemed to want to talk to him. He wondered if it was to do with his outburst at the training session. He was always envious of the casual camaraderie that people could establish with each other in the workplace. When he was teaching, he always found the staffroom intimidating. He wasn't without friendly colleagues. There were always two or three that he looked forward

172

to having a cup of tea with at break times although, come to think of it, they were probably the odd ones out, finding comfort in their own particular sub-group. Maybe he just wasn't made to be gregarious, to enjoy the easy companionship that the other teachers seemed to find in each other. Sometimes he would sit in wonder and just watch as his colleagues joked, baited and bantered each other before heading back to their classrooms. It was like watching electricity arcing between poles. Occasionally, he would get carried away with the badinage and even venture a contribution himself but it always seemed that, just as he spoke, the room would fall silent, someone would interrupt with a wittier quip or the bell would summon the end of the break and that was that.

As his teaching role diminished and he became more of an administrator, he rarely visited the staffroom. Everything he did in his job impacted on the staff but never in a positive way. He accepted that timetabling, health and safety, etc, did not enhance either his credibility or his colleagues' working experience; it could only impose more restrictions or responsibilities on them and naturally the teachers resented what they perceived as irrelevancies to the *raison d'être* of their existence.

His fellow assistants at the museum were a reasonable bunch, he had to admit. Many of the duties were of a solitary nature, especially in the galleries. You couldn't stand around chatting while someone drew a pair of glasses on the self-portrait of Augustus John. But there were opportunities to get to know each other and it seemed that a group of his colleagues met up regularly outside work but he had never been invited. Perhaps they thought him a little above them or couldn't understand why he, an ex-deputy head, would want to work in a museum. Harry didn't think he had any airs and graces. Far from it. His lunch break wasn't over when he got the message he'd been expecting.

'Harry, I overlooked the complaint of last week but this is serious.' Tim's avuncular pose of the previous week had given way to a sterner demeanour. 'What on earth got into you? Ms Rodriguez was furious when she came to see me. She's been doing manual handling for donkeys' years and she's never been spoken to like that, not even by…by…'

'…manual workers?'

'Quite. And we certainly do not expect that sort of behaviour here. Now I need to inform you that you've been invited here by way of a preliminary investigation into whether there are grounds for a disciplinary hearing into your conduct…'

'…I'll go if you want me to.'

'What?'

'I'll go. I'll resign. I don't want to be an embarrassment to the museum. It was entirely my fault. I don't know what came over me and I apologise. I'll apologise to Ms Rodriguez, of course – a written apology. But if you want my resignation today, you can have it.'

Tim had not anticipated that Harry would want to fall on his sword so easily and, although he did not quite know how to deal with Harry, there was also the fact that there was a lot of sickness amongst the staff at present and with endless school parties booked in until the end of term, it was not the best time to lose a member of staff. So Tim felt that they could resolve the situation if he accepted a warning, to which after some thought Harry agreed.

Harry didn't know if being kept on was a good thing. Frankly he couldn't care either way. As he left the museum that evening, turning up his collar in the drizzle that was falling on Cathays Park, he felt a tug on his sleeve. In the murk, he took a few seconds to recognise Meera, who usually worked the same days as him in the galleries.

'Harry, I just wanted to say about this morning. We heard you had to see Tim about it. I'm not saying you should have said what you said but she is a pompous so-and-so. We didn't think you had it in you. You were so funny. Anyway, don't take it to heart. It'll blow over. Must dash or I'll miss my bus.'

She gave his arm a squeeze and moved off. Harry watched her negotiate the puddles as she walked towards City Hall, struggling to open her umbrella.

'Thank you!' he called out finally, and Meera half-raised her arm in acknowledgement. As he made his way towards the station, head down against the buffeting wind, he could see the Christmas lights mirrored garishly in the sodden pavements. He was half thankful for the rain that now fell more strongly and masked the tears that were rolling down his cheeks.

~

Harry and Molly were seated in front of the television, she absorbed in the programme, he merely going through the motions.

'Harry, we're all going out for a drink after work next Thursday, maybe for a meal afterwards, as well. So I'll be late home. Paul's going to treat all the staff.'

'Paul?'

'Yes, Paul. He's the owner of the opticians. I've mentioned him to you before but you probably weren't listening He's such a nice chap.'

175

CHAPTER 18

Wilkins was on the phone again. Luckily Molly was at the gym.

'Harry, how are you? Just keeping you in the picture and I'd like your help. I've got some photos that I'd like you to have a look at.'

'Photos?'

'Yes, Harry, you know, those things you take with a camera. What will they think of next, eh? We've got some photos of two people and one of them might just be your Alex.'

Harry did not like the word 'your'. She was definitely not 'his' Alex. Wilkins explained that they'd managed to get CCTV images of a car matching the description of the one Guillaume had seen at the cottage. It had driven through the channel tunnel and had been caught on a camera at Maidstone Services on the M20. Harry breathed more easily. Surely the car isn't evidence of its occupants and he hadn't even seen the car.

'The thing is, two people get out of the car, a man and a woman, and go into the services. We've got some pretty good shots of them both. If one of them proves to be your Alex, we could be close to nailing this case. We've got the number plate, too, but that's a dead end. The last owner put it in part exchange but the DVLC don't have any owner after that, so that's a dead end.'

Harry's heart sank. 'How am I to view these photos? I can't drop everything and get down to Plymouth.'

'Problem solved, Harry. I've emailed them to Rumney Police Station – that's not far from you, I gather. You just need to pop over there and give my name. Today would be good.'

The desk sergeant didn't know what Harry was on about at first but he eventually found the images in someone's tray. This was only the second time Harry had been in a police station and he was still not warming to it. There were about a dozen images, mainly of the car, which Harry recognised as the Volvo that Alex had picked him up in. She's living on borrowed time, he thought, and so am I. Three images had captured the couple actually in the services – walking through the entrance, standing by the coffee shop and then leaving again. The first was very grainy. Harry thought it might be Alex but he could have been imposing his own memory of her upon the image, in the same way that he could spot Molly half a mile off just by the way she carried herself. The second image showed the woman half turned, her face in profile, looking at the man. It was Alex all right. The final image was even clearer – Alex walking straight towards the camera, naively almost, and Harry realised that in all the photos the man's face always eluded the camera. Here was the cool professional who never dropped his guard.

The policeman in the room was not aware of the turmoil in Harry's mind. He was frankly bored and couldn't understand why this bloke was taking so long over these blessed photos. You either recognise someone or you don't.

'How's it going, pal? See anyone you know there?'

Harry needed more time. He was panicking inwardly and needed to anchor his thoughts. In his head he could see the image of a stocky man trying to chase the moon across a street full of puddles. He wanted to rid his mind of it but it was there, taunting him. The man was Charles Laughton and he was trying to tell Harry something, something Harry already knew. Hobson's

Choice. He had only two courses of action - to perjure himself or to implicate himself. He had no loyalty to Alex; she had pretended to show remorse, only to drag him even further into the quicksand. But if he said nothing and she was caught, he would get dragged in anyway out of her spite.

'It's quite hard to make them out. I don't want to make a mistake.'

The policeman sighed audibly and said he would leave him to it while he got a cuppa. Harry had promised to phone Wilkins as soon as he'd seen the photos. Was there any point in putting this off? He used his mobile and Wilkins picked up straightaway.

'The photos aren't very clear but I'm pretty sure it's Alex on two of them.'

'How sure is pretty sure?'

'100 per cent.'

'Great, Harry, you're a diamond. You've just taken this investigation to a new level.'

'Do you think you can trace her?'

'Even better than that, Harry. She's in custody already. I'm coming up tomorrow to interview her.'

Dear Leonard,

That's my number up, then. Alex is in custody and whatever she may have said to me in Bristol, I reckon I'm for the chop. Once the police start questioning her, I think she'll confess readily to her involvement because she wants to minimise the impact on her stepdaughter, who has no one to support her. But by coming clean in the hope of a lighter sentence, she might be tempted to implicate me more. Who knows, I might end up as the person who masterminded the crime. You think I'm getting paranoid about all this, don't you?

Whatever happens, there's no way that this can be kept secret from Molly now. Either I tell her or she'll know soon enough from the police. I can picture the scene. The whole family's going to be together this Christmas. Everyone will be seated around the dining table, full of festive cheer and stuffed to the gills with turkey and all the trimmings, when the doorbell will announce the arrival of the boys in blue complete with handcuffs. My grandson, seated in his little highchair, will be left with an abiding memory of Christmas centred around a confusing image of Santa Claus arriving with flashing blue lights and wearing a big helmet.

CHAPTER 19

Harry couldn't understand why Molly wanted a real tree this Christmas. They had managed with the artificial one for years, ever since the children had left home. It was a bit tatty but once you'd covered with it with lights and baubles it looked fine. But this year, with Molly planning a family Christmas, a real tree would be more atmospheric for Billy.

'Billy doesn't know a tree from a lamppost. He's just a baby.'

Molly gave Harry one of her withering stares and the matter was settled.

When the children were young, the getting of the tree was a major event. The four of them would pile into Harry's car and, because the tree had to go on the roof, this meant putting on the roof rack, ensuring there was plenty of rope and, even though the forestry was only a short a drive away, carrying two pieces of red cloth as hazard warnings for the tree when it was loaded.

'I don't think the police are going to stop us for transporting a Christmas tree,' Molly would say. 'It's not as if we're the only ones doing it at this time of year.'

'Safety first,' Harry would say, and that was that.

In fact the only danger the tree ever caused was one Christmas when a piece of red cloth blew off the top of Harry's car onto the windscreen of the car behind. Harry was forced to stop and apologise to the driver who was trying to disentangle it from his windscreen wipers. Later that evening Hazel asked Molly the meaning of the word the driver had called Daddy and Molly had to be very inventive in satisfying her daughter's curiosity.

Harry didn't object to real Christmas trees. He rather liked them in fact. It was the extra tension they caused at an already stressful time of the year. It began as soon as they had reached the forestry. It was usually raining and full of other families making the same trip. Hundreds of trees of all shapes and sizes would be lying around and it was Harry's job to find a tree and hold it upright by the top so that Molly could inspect it. The tree had to be the right height and shape, and be uniformly foliaged, so that whichever way Harry turned it for Molly's scrutiny there would be no visible gaps within the branches. It didn't matter how many times Harry posed with a tree, it would not meet the exacting standards that Molly had in her mind's eye. Harry knew that Molly's tree only inhabited Christmas books and cards. It did not exist in reality. Sometimes it was like the Judgement of Paris and Molly would narrow it down to three trees, with Harry trying to hold up one while keeping an eye on the other two so that they weren't whisked away by other families. By this time the children were cold and fed up, the magic gone, and Molly would make the decision that this was the one, although she always knew that the perfect tree – the primus inter pares of Christmas trees - was still calling to her from underneath a mountain of trees that the advancing darkness prevented them from exploring. But as he tied the chosen tree on the roof rack, Harry knew that once it was taken home, wrenched from its woodland habitat, it would cease to be the magical tree that Molly craved and become the stunted, misshapen, gap-filled tree that Harry had rushed her into choosing.

This year Molly was going to leave the tree entirely to Harry and he decided, for simplicity's sake, to go not to the forestry but to a local greengrocer's that always had a fair selection and at a reasonable price. He chose a tree without too much fuss and was strapping it to the car when he noticed that he had parked opposite the optician's where Molly worked and, in fact, where she was working today. He pondered about going in and saying hello, but something held him back, and he thought better of it. The road was a cul-de-sac and so he had to go to the end to turn. As he was coming past the optician's he saw Molly getting into a large Audi, the door of which was being held open by a young man. In light of recent suspicions about his wife's behaviour, this was very alarming. His instinct was to wait up the road until the car had passed and then follow it. But he realised that following in a car with a Christmas tree on top might be rather conspicuous. He drove home quickly, left the car in the drive with the tree on top and phoned the optician's. He had just missed Molly, he was told. It was her half-day. She never worked on Wednesday afternoon. This was news to Harry because she always came in at tea time.

This was intolerable. How could Molly be so blatant? Where might they have gone? Harry then remembered something that Molly had said one evening when he was engrossed in a documentary. An image by Tomasso da Modena had flashed onto the screen and it contained a figure in spectacles, one of the earliest known images depicting eye-glasses. Molly had glanced up from her book and said, 'You should have been an optician, Harry. I've never seen a poor one and we could be living in …' Now what address had she said? He searched the depths of his memory – Cyncoed Road; maybe somewhere in leafy Lisvane; no, it was Lakeside, but where? Then it hit him. Cefn-Coed Drive. She had said Cefn-Coed Drive. As he drove off, having taken off the Christmas tree, Harry realised that he was consumed by feelings that were new to him and they

182

were not just emotional. He felt physically sick, his stomach was in knots, his mouth was dry and his temples were pounding. When he finally turned into Cefn-Coed Drive, he realised he had no idea of the route he had taken. He drove slowly down in the direction of the Lake and sure enough there was a black Audi parked on the large gravelled driveway of a substantial detached house.

Harry parked his car by the Lake and walked up Cefn-Coed Drive. He didn't know what he intended to do but he was compelled to do something. The house stood well back from the road, with large fir trees almost masking it from the road. He could just about reach the front door without anyone witnessing his approach. He checked the Audi and there was no doubt that it was the same car he'd seen Molly get in. The bonnet was still warm. The gravel crunched noisily as he walked towards the front door. He had still not worked out what he was going to do but to do nothing was the sign of a coward, a cuckold. For once in his life, he had to act rather than think. He had just reached the edge of the cover afforded by the trees when the front door opened and out stepped the man he had seen with Molly. The man went to the boot and brought out an attaché case. He seemed in a very animated mood - as well he might, thought Harry, with my wife inside. Harry continued walking. The man shut the boot of the car and, turning to head back into the house, glimpsed Harry for the first time. He looked at Harry enquiringly as if he was a tradesman coming to collect his money. Harry knew that this was his moment. He had to assume control but at all costs keep his dignity.

Having formed these thoughts in his mind, Harry lunged at the man and attempted a blow to the head. The man merely sidestepped Harry's haymaker and, still holding the case in one hand, landed a stinging upper-cut to Harry's cheekbone, sending him sprawling. Even in his dazed state, Harry realised that this was not the outcome he had imagined. Lying on his back, he squinted at the man through his good eye and saw him take out his mobile. But before punching in 999 the man looked down at Harry and said: 'Good Lord, it's Mr Dymond!'

~

Harry was sitting in a large kitchen, cradling a cup of coffee in his hands, slightly shaking, while his cheekbone throbbed painfully.

'Look, I can't say again how sorry I am. You just came at me and I acted out of instinct. I didn't recognise you at first. I don't normally go about thumping my old teachers. Let me put some ice on your cheek.'

Harry did not resist. He was too far gone and he had a feeling that something had gone horribly wrong but he couldn't work it out. All he knew was that the person before him was Paul Nuttall whom he had taught nearly thirty years ago.

'Listen, Mr Dymond, this may sound bizarre but can I ask if this has anything to do with your wife? I didn't know until today who she was. I just know her as Molly. My wife Jenny runs the optician's; I just nip in now and again. Then today I offered Molly a lift to the gym because it was on my way and we got talking. She mentioned her husband used to teach at the comp and it clicked who she was. And then you appear and try to land one on me. It's a bizarre coincidence. So, what is going on, Mr Dymond?'

Harry remembered him, of course. Paul was a thin, weedy boy who wasn't interested in history but was always an affable and undemanding kid to teach.

'I don't know what to say. I've made a terrible mistake. I saw you and Molly getting into your car and made the worst conclusion anyone could arrive at.'

'Mr Dymond, that would make you an extremely jealous man if all it takes is seeing another man with your wife. I would have to be extremely blatant to have an affair with one of my wife's employees.'

Harry removed the ice pack from his cheek to speak.

'I'm not a jealous man. At least, I've never been a jealous man until recently. I'm afraid it's all a bit confused. I've got a lot on my plate at the moment and I can't think staright. I'm afraid I've got the wrong end of a very large stick. Oh my God, what's going to happen to Molly now? She's not to blame here. What about her job?'

'Look, Mr Dymond, Jenny took Molly on and from what I hear they get on really well together. Jenny talks about her a lot. She's great with the customers and I'm sure Jenny has no wish to see her go. As you so rightly say, this has got nothing to do with her. But there's something wrong here and you've got to sort it out for Molly's sake. If you think Molly's the kind of woman who would have an affair, you don't know you wife. I'll tell you what I'll do. I won't say anything to Jenny, but I will expect you to come clean with Molly or otherwise she'll get to know about it, because she doesn't deserve all this nonsense.'

Paul saw Harry to the door.

'You were a good teacher, Mr Dymond. History wasn't my cup of tea. I was always keener on maths and science but you worked hard with me and you were always fair. I know some of the kids would give you stick but I think we all knew that you were trying your best.'

'How did you get into the optician business?'

185

'Easy ride there. My father set up the business and it was natural that when I left university I should join him. He had just the one shop, where your wife works, but we worked well together and opened two more branches. That's what I do really, flit around and make sure the finances in order.'

'And your father?'

'He died about ten years ago. In the last few years he'd left me very much to my own devices. He could see that the business was in safe hands. It left him to carry on with other things. He loved his golf but his passion was sports cars. He built up quite a collection before he died. Wait a second, I'll show you'

They were walking past the double garage that was set to the side of the house. Paul fumbled in his pocket and took out a set of keys. He blipped them in the direction of the garage and the sound of a motor whirred as the two large white doors opened upward. Paul stepped inside and switched on a fluorescent light. It stuttered into life and finally filled the space with a white light that brought the contents of the garage into sharp definition. Two cars occupied the garage, unequal in size. On the right was a magnificent Series 1 E-Type Jaguar in racing green, its long bonnet facing forward, a classic machine that would increase the heartbeat of any enthusiast. But Harry was staring at the smaller vehicle, tiny by comparison with its neighbour. It was an MG Midget with a familiar registration number: JOE 679C.

Dear Leonard,

I thought my life was complicated enough but the Gods above want to test me even further. I am fortunate not to be on an assault charge. I can see the headline now: TEACHER ATTACKS FORMER PUPIL. What was I doing? I'm lucky he didn't kill me. He's at least half a foot taller than me. He's being very gracious about the whole thing.

I've got to get myself together. All this stems from Alex and that stupid bloody package. I can't think about anything else. I'm all in a daze and not thinking straight. My mind feels a snow globe. Everything is swirling around and that's the worst scenario for my sanity. I need to restore some kind of order or I'm going to lose it completely. And to complicate matters further, that MG has turned up, large as life and twice as shiny, as if it has just emerged from the showroom.

Okay. Deep breath. I need to quantify the problems that beset me, then prioritise them and finally deal with them one by one. If I can eliminate some of them, the rest may become more manageable. There, I'm beginning to feel better already. You see, Leonard, I told you that talking to you helps. Right. So, in no particular order, o what can ail thee, knight in arms?

- I have been unfaithful to Molly with another woman (overstated, perhaps, but Molly will see it that way);
- I definitely touched Alex inappropriately;
- I may have committed a criminal act in carrying that package;
- If not, I have compromised my innocence by meeting Alex;
- A dangerous criminal has threatened me if I expose Alex;

187

- He thinks I know too much, even though I don't, and may come after me anyway just in case;
- I am keeping information from Wilkins, which betrays the apparent trust he has in me;
- Molly may be having an affair with someone called Paul;
- I have stupidly attacked the wrong Paul;
- The wrong Paul is an ex-pupil and Molly's boss;
- Molly knows nothing of most of the above and will probably divorce me when she finds out and move in with said Paul;
- Whatever she does, my silence is a betrayal of our relationship;
- I have made a pig's ear of things at the museum and am close to losing my job;
- The fate of Joe and the MG is small beer comparatively but it still dogs me, and now the car has turned up!

What do you think, Leonard? Have I omitted anything? The list is longer than I thought and I don't know where I should start. The obvious thing to do is to tell Molly everything. The problems will get worse if she learns from another source but I'm afraid to tell her for fear of her reaction. I don't want to lose her. It would finish me.

CHAPTER 20

Harry and Molly were sitting opposite each other in the kitchen, the dinner plates cleared, the pudding postponed for a few minutes to allow the lasagne to settle. Harry had refreshed Molly's glass and was thinking about opening another bottle.

'Do you remember,' said Molly, 'that brooch you broke, the one my grandmother gave me? We were in our first flat in Grangetown.'

Harry mumbled an acknowledgement with an enquiring look.

'You stepped on it by accident and snapped the clasp. It was my fault actually because I must have dropped it on the bedroom floor. You knew how I treasured that brooch and you panicked. Instead of just coming clean about it, you hid it away in the car. I think you intended to get it fixed but you wanted to buy some time and you weren't sure how much it would cost. We were always hard up in those days. But I missed the brooch straightaway and we spent all day taking the flat apart, every drawer, every cupboard, every corner, but of course we were never going to find it. I knew I'd seen the brooch recently and I rarely wore it anyway, so I knew that if it wasn't in the flat it must have been stolen. We had a creepy landlord and we suspected that he came into the flat when we were at work. There were telltale signs, if you remember – a muddy footprint on the lino or my underwear drawer in disarray. And so I decided to go to the police and you got into a right old flap, arguing that we had no proof and we were bound to get into trouble. And then I knew from your face that you had the answer to the missing brooch because, if the landlord had nothing to do with it, it had to be you. I was reunited with the brooch, you explained what had happened and in the end the repair didn't break the bank.'

'Why are you bringing all this up now? It was a long time ago.'

'When we talked about it at the time, we agreed that from then on we would have no secrets from each other. We would always be open and honest with each other - apart from the price of handbags, of course - because secrets have a way of driving wedges between people and we can't afford that to happen to us.'

Harry now opened a new bottle of wine, as he reckoned they both might need it by the end of the evening.

'The thing is, Harry, there's been something eating away at you ever since you came back from France. You're not good at expressing your feelings at the best of times but you're even worse at hiding them. I know there's something bothering you because you're even more distracted than usual. And then the other day, you appear with this great big bruise on you face, claiming that you walked into a door. So, clearly something's up and I hate to see you in this silent distress.'

Harry didn't know where to begin. He could have given Molly chapter and verse about recent events at the museum and about his encounter with Paul Nuttall but they seemed nothing by comparison with events in France.

'Okay, I admit that there are things happening but one of them involves you. Something did happen in France and I'll come clean about it but only if you do the same. Agreed?'

'Harry, you're being positively intriguing!' But Molly saw the seriousness on Harry's face. 'Sorry, I'm listening.'

Harry told Molly everything that had happened in France and after. She listened without interrupting, the only sound in the kitchen being Harry's voice and the ticking of the clock. When he had finished, he took a long pull on his wine glass and Molly could see the beads of sweat on his forehead. She had many questions and they could have been asked in any order but she chose one that was already causing her stomach to tighten.

'Did you want to sleep with this Alex?'

Harry wasn't surprised at the question and he didn't really care about the consequences of his reply. He knew that telling the truth would distress Molly but he was weighed down by such secrets and anxieties that he needed to unburden himself at whatever cost.

'Yes, I did, but I know now how stupid that would have been.'

He stared hard at Molly and could see the uncertainty etched upon a face that was normally so composed.

'You see, Molly, men think about other women all the time. It's part of their make-up. But it usually remains an unfulfilled fantasy. It serves a purpose of convincing us of the fiction that if we had the opportunity women would fall at our feet. It's just a male thing. Sometimes men will make that fantasy a reality but then you're on a slippery slope. I've never been alone in that way with another woman. But it was a physical desire – a fantasy made flesh, if you like, and it was being alone with her in those circumstances. Suddenly everything became possible and I was feeling low, I was feeling down, with you not being there. But it was a temptation only. I didn't sleep with her but if we are both to be honest, I wanted to.'

'So what happens now? With the police, I mean.'

'Alex has confessed to her part in the crime – the police phoned me today - but they're no nearer to finding this guy. He's a slippery character who could be anywhere, England, France or maybe trying his luck in another country. As for me, the police say that because I cooperated in identifying Alex they don't think it's likely I'll be called to give evidence. It might have been different if Alex had denied any involvement, but she's come clean and she's told them how I was tricked into becoming an unwitting mule. That's an apt description in so many ways. Wilkins says that Alex will hopefully get a lighter sentence when it all comes to court.'

'Do you want to see Alex again?

Harry tightened his fingers around the stem of the wine glass and might have snapped it.

'No, she used me and even though she was acting under duress at the end I can't forgive her for that. Molly, I just want things to be back to normal. I did something stupid over there and the whole thing got out of control. One minute I'm agreeing to take a parcel and the next I'm involved in organised crime, with the possibility of being convicted for handling goods. I've been really scared, you know.'

Molly smiled.

'What's so funny?'

'Well, you're Mr Steady, Mr Cautious. You map out every minute of your day so that you're always in control. If I ask you to come to the shops with me, you have to consult a spreadsheet because you can't do spontaneity. I let you go to France on your own and you get involved in international smuggling. I'm not letting you out of my sight any more.'

'Is that true? Haven't you got your sights on someone else? Where does Paul fit into this?

'Paul. What Paul? Do you mean Paul at the optician's? He's married for goodness sake. I work with his wife.'

At the mention of Paul's name, Harry's cheekbone gave him an involuntary twinge of pain.

'You know who I mean. I'm talking about the Paul on your mobile, the guy who phoned you that day, the guy you spend so much time with. Are you going to deny it?'

Molly's face suddenly lit up with realisation and Harry knew that he had finally hit the spot. She took a sip of wine and breathed deeply.

'Okay, Harry, I'll tell you about Paul. But first let me tell you the background. This is all about being a middle-aged woman, which - pardon me for saying - is different from being a middle aged man. Men seem to move through the ageing process in a fairly straightforward way. You're young, you get married, be a father, develop a paunch, go down the pub, your hair thins a bit, you watch sport, you start snoring, you wear garish tee-shirts that you think are trendy and you arrive at the train stop called middle age relatively unscathed and all this happens at a steady pace, so steady you hardly notice it.

'It's different for woman and, yes, I would say that, wouldn't I? But a woman's role is still primarily to do with nest building and child bearing. When I was young I was up for women's equality and we still haven't achieved it but I didn't want any man to take over my role as a mother. I loved having kids and I regret not having more. I know that we talked it through and it was the right thing at the time for you to have the snip but I still regret not having a bigger family. I loved every minute about being a mother because I was wanted and needed. My love for Christopher and Hazel was unconditional and their love for me was the same. And you showed me your love but in different ways, in providing when the children were young, in loving me physically because that showed me you found me attractive, in helping me around the house in your particular way. It all validated me as a woman and I loved it. It was the happiest time of my life.

'I know that we have children and love and care for them so that they can become independent and leave home but sometimes that sounds like the cruellest of arrangements. *Love me, care for me, teach me, strengthen me and, before I forget, bye!!* Women never get over the wrench of seeing their children leave them. They accept it as a natural consequence of being a good mother but physically you never get over it. Sometimes I ache for our two. I physically ache for them. I may be sitting on the sofa and I suddenly think of those times when we would be huddled together reading a story or just laughing at something silly. But here's the rub, Harry. Just at the time when you're coping with the loss of your children, the loves of your life, nature says: oh by the way I'm going to divest you of the traces of your womanhood, the thing you hold so dear. And this isn't going to be a slow, gradual process. I'm going to give you hell – hot flushes, sweats, heavy periods. I'm going to send your hormones on a switchback around your body so that your moods are all over the place. And by the way, that body of yours, the one that made you an attractive female of the species, I'm going to change it. I'm going to relax your muscles so that everything goes south, I'm going to thicken your waistline and stick a few pounds on your bum. In short, I'm going to make you feel deeply unattractive about yourself.

'The thing is, Harry, men wouldn't go through what women have to tolerate. You'd be saying *hang on, this*

194

isn't right, we need a better system than this. Men wouldn't queue endlessly in toilets as women do. They'd just say this isn't working, let's build some more toilets.

'I'm know I'm going on, Harry, but I'm nearly there now. I paid less attention to all this when I was working full time because I felt fulfilled and I liked my job. But since we retired and I've got more time to myself, I've realise that I want to feel better about myself. I want to feel like a woman again before it's too late and if I don't do it now I never will. So I joined the gym with Angela but she suggested that we could speed everything up if we got a personal trainer. We could share the cost, too. That's where Paul comes in...'

'...Paul's your personal trainer?'

'Yes, but let me finish. So Angela and I started at the gym with him. Then he suggested going for runs and at this point Angela started to cry off. I think it was getting too much for her so I've tended to have him on my own, which is great because Angela was slowing me down. Paul's a good-looking thirty-something with abs like steel and a bum to die for. But he not only bats for the other side, he opens the innings. So, I am not likely to be led astray. Mystery solved, I think.'

'But why were you so secretive about him?'

'For the simple reason that you've never believed in gyms and all that stuff. You think women only go there for a gossip and to show off a snazzy outfit. I thought if I told you I'd gone further and engaged a personal trainer you would belittle me. I've been going to the gym for weeks but you never comment on the results.'

'I have noticed. I think you're looking great.'

'Go on then, tell me. How do I look great?'

'Well, you look thinner, I mean slimmer. Um, your figure is very shapely these days, very shapely. Your bust is …more taut and your bottom is …pert. You look much better than you used to.'

'Pert. You're a star turn. Only you could use the word *pert*. Do you want pudding?'

'No, I'm still full after the lasagne. We can have it tomorrow.'

'Well,' said Molly, leaning over and kissing his cheek, 'I think an early night might be nice, don't you?'

CHAPTER 21

If confession is good for the soul, Harry was thinking of turning Catholic. He felt altogether lighter, as if a heavy rucksack of emotion had been lifted from his shoulders. It was Sunday and Molly was in town doing battle with the Christmas crowds. Harry was having a cup of coffee in the kitchen, looking vaguely through the French doors as the last leaves of the sycamore drifted slowly to earth. It had been an unusual autumn with everyone commenting on the vibrancy of the foliage – the leaves in the parks and gardens all bright yellow, deep red or burnished bronze. People talked of a harsh winter to come, the abundant berries being evidence of Nature's bountiful insurance against the cold weather to come.

As it was a dry day, Harry decided to give an hour to clearing the leaves around the patio and was just about to gather up his tools when the phone rang. In recent weeks the phone had been his demon but today he felt relaxed as he picked up the receiver. It was Wilkins.

'Harry, I've got some bad news, I'm afraid. Alex is dead.'

Harry felt a cold chill descend from his head to his stomach and flopped down on a kitchen chair. The receipt of grave news in familiar surroundings is a feeling of immediate and jarring unreality and he felt it now.

Wilkins related how Alex had been released on bail. She had told the police the whole story but had refused to identify Jean-Luc. She had gone back to Witney where she hoped to continue running her shop. Her stepdaughter had been fantastic in her absence, Wilkins said, and the shop was just about making ends meet. Whatever happened to Alex at her trial, they would carry on with the business. Last night the two of them had spent the evening in The Eagle, a pub in the centre of Witney. They'd got back to the flat they shared above the shop in Corn Street around 11.30. About 3.00am a fire broke out in the back room of the shop and quickly engulfed the building, raging through the shop itself, which was full of combustible materials. The fire service arrived quickly and tried to get to the first-floor flat, which bystanders said was occupied. It was impossible. When the firemen finally gained access they found two badly-burned bodies at the top of the stairs.

'So, were they were trying to escape and got overcome by fumes?' asked Harry.

'Looks like it,' said Wilkins. 'The fire service were immediately suspicious because of how quickly the fire spread. They're still investigating but they've found traces of an accelerant, petrol most likely, in the back room and at the bottom of the stairs. They're pretty sure the fire was started deliberately and we can guess who that might be. I think this Jean-Luc fellow was getting jumpy and thought that Alex was going to shop him. He couldn't trust her to keep silent so he killed her and he couldn't care less if the stepdaughter died as well. He's a ruthless bastard, that one, but the trouble is we're no nearer to finding him. He covers his tracks every time he makes a move.'

Harry had little he could say to Wilkins but he felt ashamed that a feeling of self-preservation formed in his mind. What if this ruthless bastard came after him?

'I don't think so, Harry. You never met him or saw him. Alex only ever gave you a name and that was likely to be false, as hers was. You have nothing that would identify him or incriminate him. He's done all he needs to do. He's cleared the decks, as it were. It's a sad end to this whole business. I interviewed Alex and she was no career criminal. I think she was out of her depth and only kept going because she was scared of this Jean-Luc. She couldn't get out of his grip. And do you know what? I think she only decided to hand herself in because she couldn't live with herself after involving you. That pricked her conscience. She said as much at interview. She said she was ashamed of using you.'

Harry told Molly of Alex's death when she returned from shopping.

'I can only say how sad that is, that someone could have so little regard for another human's life and to kill the daughter, too. But it's over, Harry, and you've got to move on. You had nothing to do with Alex's death. You just got dragged into this whole messy business but you're out now. And Wilkins is right. You've got nothing that this Jean-Luc wants; so you're safe.'

In making his 'confession' the night before Harry had missed one small but significant detail – the photos taken in Bristol – and now they were beginning to haunt him. Wilkins could say that Alex had told him nothing about Jean-Luc but did Jean-Luc know this? If he could kill an innocent girl, then what did he care about the niceties of this situation? He did not seem to be a man who deliberated overmuch about whether someone did or did not know his identity. There was also something else gnawing away at Harry's mind. It was an unresolved thing clicking away in the synapses of his brain, a half-forgotten word or words that had something to do with Alex and would not go away. It was like a missing link in a chain or the hand of a clock that shudders but can't move on until you change the battery. He knew it was important but he just couldn't recollect it.

Dear Leonard,

This whole affair is spinning out of control. I thought that, with Alex doing the decent thing and admitting to the police that I had been duped into getting involved in this sorry business, I was off the hook. Wilkins said as much himself. I'd also squared everything with Molly and, bless her, she'd forgiven me. But now Alex is dead! Why would anyone want to kill Alex and her stepdaughter, for goodness sake? I mean, what is it with this Jean-Luc? Is he some kind of psychopath?

I keep thinking of Alex desperately trying to escape from that burning flat. What a terrible way to die, to find that you are trapped in a raging inferno and there is no escape. I just hope she and Emily were overcome by the smoke and did not have to suffer the agony of being burned alive.

I was angry with Alex and that anger was partly fuelled by the fact that she used me and made a fool of me. I felt humiliated by the way she had played with my emotions and abused my good nature. But I was beginning to see that, like me, she was also a victim, in her case a victim of Jean-Luc who took advantage of her pressing need to keep her business afloat. What she did was wrong but, when life has got you by the throat, who am I to judge her? I think she acted out of character and was blinded for a time to the true nature of what she was doing. Maybe she thought that smuggling these maps and books was a victimless crime. I think of those bankers whose actions have caused greater suffering than anything Alex did and they're not all in prison.

Look at what I did lately. I get a notion in my head that Molly is being unfaithful. I have no evidence for this. I could have asked her about this Paul on her mobile. But what do I do instead? I misread every sign of her secrecy about the personal trainer and build it into a huge edifice of jealousy. I throw all reason and logic out of the window and for the first time in my life I let my emotions dictate my actions. What if I had actually thumped Paul and he had fallen against his car, cracked his skull and died? By acting out of character, I would find myself charged with manslaughter. I am no better than Alex and that is why her death affects me so. She has paid the harshest of penalties for what she did.

But it gets worse, doesn't it? Wilkins doesn't know that Jean-Luc may be after me. If he can kill Alex and Emily, then I'm just a snail under his boot. I want to say to Jean-Luc: I have no information about you. Alex told me nothing. I cannot identify you. You are a man of complete mystery to me and I would like it to remain that way. Perhaps he just wants to scare me and, if that's all he wants to do, he's certainly making a good job of it.

Maybe I'm just being paranoid about Jean-Luc. Surely, if he wanted to harm me, he would have done something by now. I may getting into a panic about nothing. Maybe I should tell Wilkins... but not just now.

CHAPTER 22

Harry crunched over the familiar gravel but this time without apprehension. Paul was in the garage polishing the E-Type as if he was applying lotion to a baby's skin.

'I promised my father I'd take care of his beloved cars. It's a chore but a promise is a promise. How's your cheekbone? I still can't get over…'

'…It's fine, can't feel anything at all. You said you had some information about the Midget.'

'Yes,' Paul replied as he went to the back of the garage and returned with a sheaf of papers, 'my father always kept meticulous records of his cars – log books, service records, photos, all the various car club ralleys he attended. He even raced this one,' patting the Jaguar, 'in the Le Mans Classique. Didn't come anywhere, but he was so proud of competing and it's all documented.'

Harry cast his mind back and remembered that Paul's father would often pick up his son at the end of a term in one of his precious sports cars and there was an almost palpable whiff of testosterone emanating from fathers and sons who would crowd around the vehicle in a scrum of male bonding.

'Anyway, there's not so much on the Midget but it's all here. You're welcome to borrow these papers.' He handed Harry a manila folder with the car's registration number carefully written on the front.

'Mr Dymond, can I ask about Molly? It's not my business, I know, but how are things between you?'

'Please call me Harry. I feel old when you call me Mr Dymond. Things are fine between Molly and me. She doesn't know about the …eh, incident but everything's fine. Thank you for being so discreet.'

'That's not a problem. Actually, I've got something to ask you, a sort of favour, but I'll understand if you don't want to do it. It's my boy, Ralph; he's doing his GCSEs next summer. He's not an academic and he's struggling in a few subjects but particularly history. Would you be interested in giving him some coaching, for payment naturally, just to give him a bit of confidence? But I quite understand if you feel you can't.'

Harry hesitated but with a half-smile said: 'I'd be delighted. Let me have the name of the syllabus he's doing and some of his work. I'm free most evenings if that suits you.'

'Thank you, Mr …thank you, Harry. I'm sure the two of you will get along famously. He's a quiet lad but is always eager to please.'

Harry walked back to his car with the sheaf of papers in his hand. He knew he could have said no to tutoring Ralph but the prospect actually pleased him and he was conscious that this might go some way to squaring the debt that he owed to Paul's discretion. He got into his car and drove off down to the Lake. He was wondering if his worksheets were still up to date and therefore didn't notice the black BMW following him at a safe distance.

CHAPTER 23

Paul's records of the Midget revealed little of interest. Paul's father had meticulously restored the vehicle in the 1990s but the years prior to that time were unaccounted for. Harry knew that the car had languished in Mr Barker's garage for years. However, the original logbook was in the bundle and the name of Joseph Barker was listed there. It was at least proof that part of Harry's theory was correct. This had to be Mr Barker's son. Harry made a few notes and decided to put the papers in a safe place before returning them to Paul. Molly had a habit of sweeping up anything that lay on a coffee table or worktop for more than a respectable time and stuffing it anywhere, which infuriated Harry. He kept a bedside drawer clear for this purpose and that's where he was going to put the papers now. But something already in the drawer caught his eye. It was the guest book from the cottage. He knew that he needed to look through the book once more, for something that was faintly calling to him but he didn't know what.

He flipped through the pages again, skimming through the comments left by this year's guests. What was he looking for? And then he came to the October entry –Alex's comments – and read them aloud:

'Had a lovely week in this beautiful cottage – so quaint! The motte in Bréllidy is worth a visit and there's a lovely riverside walk in La Roch Derrien. Good shopping in Guingemp and Lanion. Best beaches we found were at Trégasstel, Plomanac'h and Perross Guirec. If you're looking for seafood, try the restaurants around the port in Paimpoll but the perfect place for a spot of lunch is at the Casino in St Quay Potrieux. The restaurant overlooks the beach. Good market in Tréguer on Wednesdays. Enjoy!'

Harry remembered glancing at the entry in the guest book when he was in the cottage. He didn't have the time then to absorb what now looked so clearly odd. All the placenames were misspelled, which if written by Alex was frankly very strange because she was a fluent French speaker and what was even odder was that she had still put in the acute accent in Brélidy and Trégastel, and the apostrophe in Ploumanac'h. How could she have made such glaring mistakes in the name of every single place she visited? But had she really visited all these places in a week when, by her own account, she and Jean-Luc were holed up in the cottage awaiting the delivery of illicit goods? And then Harry realised that Alex's comments merely parodied the visitors' guide that he and Molly had put together to recommend places to guests. Alex had visited none of these places.

So why write a spurious account of a week spent in the Côtes d'Armor? All this subterfuge served no purpose, unless she was just ensuring that their stay at the cottage looked as normal as possible. But surely she could have managed that without the spelling mistakes. How could she have made so many of them? Was there some kind of method in her madness? And then he noticed that she had actually signed her entry with a false name: Jack Hughes. Why on earth did she need to do that? Jack Hughes, of all the names to pick. He spoke the name softly to himself, *Jack Hughes....Jack Hughes*. And suddenly it was as if all his arteries had made one massive combined effort to flood his brain with oxygen and light up the deepest corner of his memory. Alex was giving him the sign he needed.

Harry began picking out the misspelled words. Was there a pattern here? He scrutinised the errors again - an extra 'L' in Brélidy, a missing 'E' in La Roche Derrien, an 'E' instead of an 'A' in Guingamp. He wrote every erroneous letter down on a piece of paper:

L E A N S U S L R I

It made no sense at all. He wrote down different combinations on the paper but got nowhere. Exasperated, Harry went onto the landing and pulled down the loft ladder. He climbed clumsily up into the attic, switching on the light as he went. Now where was it? Amidst the jumble of boxes were some of the children's old board games. Ludo, Guess Who? and Snakes and Ladders. And at the bottom of the pile lay a battered Scrabble box. This would make it easier. Harry opened the lid and took out those tiles that matched the ten letters he was trying to fathom. He scattered them randomly on the chipboard floor to see if a pattern emerged.

His first attempt gave him LIAR UNLESS. Unless what? he thought. Then there was ALIEN SLURS, followed by SNAIL RULES and LUNAR ISLES. This was getting him nowhere and a glance at his watch told him that Molly would be home from work soon. He didn't want her to find him doing something surreptitious in the loft, now that things were better between them.

He tried the letters again for what seemed the twentieth time and something began to emerge, still somewhat jumbled, but beginning to give up something comprehensible. He moved one or two letters and then sat back, astonished.

Harry dashed down from the loft, almost missing his footing. Fumbling for a card in his pocket, he dialled the number on it.

'Hello, I need to speak to Detective Sergeant Wilkins urgently. It's very important.'

CHAPTER 24

Harry was strolling rather aimlessly through the French Impressionists, still wrestling in his mind with what the letters had revealed. Wilkins had said he would get back to him as soon as he had anything concrete but that, thanks to Harry, he thought that the final pieces of the jigsaw would soon be in place. The gallery was unusually quiet, with visitors shunning artistic enlightenment for the baser pleasures of cramming in some last minute Christmas shopping. Harry didn't mind having the place almost to himself. The solitude gave him time to ponder on the twists and turns of the whole affair. He was still saddened by Alex's death, the senselessness of a life so brutally cut short and that of her stepdaughter who had been entirely innocent in the whole business. But he was feeling relieved that no more threatening messages had come his way. Perhaps now he could get on with his life, not an easy task in itself, but made easier now that the threat of criminal prosecution and physical harm from 'Jean-Luc' seemed to be receding. He was also thinking about Molly and the way she had handled Harry's behaviour in France. Not many wives would have been so understanding. And now that both of them had revealed their particular secrets, the atmosphere between them was improving. The silences that grow between a couple are like a desert spreading into a temperate forest. The process is slow but unrelenting and before you know it the forest has been reduced to mere oases separated by miles of arid waste.

He was still musing on all of this when a man burst into the gallery. In fact, so absorbed was Harry in his reverie that he failed to notice him at first. And then he saw the gun pointed at him. What few visitors there had been in the gallery scattered sharply but with commendable silence for a museum, leaving a stunned Harry to face the man alone.

Harry's senses were slow to kick in as he tried to evaluate the incongruity of a gunman in the Impressionists' gallery. The man was short, stocky and, Harry noticed, sweating profusely, a consequence perhaps of wearing a bulky overcoat on such a mild day? Perhaps not. These observations were made in a split second as Harry realised that he needed to react in a positive way. What had they said on the training day in the 'Dealing With Emergencies' section? Remember the three Cs he'd been told. Keep CALM, take CONTROL and …? Harry had forgotten the third C. And this was a situation that his commendable knowledge of art history was unlikely to defuse.

It was the gunman who took control. 'Shut those doors, lock 'em if they'll lock. Use your radio to tell them that no one enters this room or it goes up. Got it?'

The man opened his overcoat and Harry could see the makeshift vest with its bulky tightness and protruding wires. He felt the blood drain out of him and his limbs go floppy. He just managed to lower himself onto a bench in front of Renoir's 'La Parisienne' rather than collapse in an unseemly heap.

'Do it!' barked the gunman. 'Do it now!'

Harry got back up and quickly radioed the message but news had already spread and everyone seemed to be aware that a 'Dealing With Emergencies' situation was unfolding. Harry was able to blurt out that the man was a bomber before his radio was snatched from him.

'Now listen. Nobody makes a move or this gallery goes sky high. When the police arrive, they can speak to me on this radio.'

Harry had rarely felt real fear in his life but he felt it now. He was struggling to control his breathing and to calm himself. He needed to focus on something to restore his equilibrium. A memory flashed across his consciousness. He was about six or seven and was playing on his own in the lane at the back of his house. He seemed to be on his own a lot as a child. He had some sort of headgear on – Indian feathers maybe, no it was a Davy Crockett hat. They were the must-have item back then for any self-respecting frontiersman in Torrington. He was stalking a bear just like his hero, *killed him a b'ar when he was only three*, as the song went. He was carrying a stick that he had found in the lane but it was really Davy Crockett's rifle. He came stealthily through the gate into his back garden where he could see his father hoeing the vegetable patch. His father had no idea that his son was creeping up behind him and Harry did not know of the demons that his father carried around in his head. This is great fun, thought Harry. With every step he expected his father to wheel around and catch him but he didn't. Harry's heart was thumping as he poked the stick softly into his father's back. 'Hands up, pardner, I got the drop on you.' But the words were only half said because Harry's father spun round in an instant, hoe still in his hands, and if Harry had been three inches taller he would have killed him with the flaying weapon. But it wasn't the hoe that frightened Harry, it was his father's eyes, wide and glaring, his teeth clenched, the lips pulled back, like a rabid dog about to pounce. This was not Harry's father, not the man who would carry Harry on his shoulders when he met him from work at the end of the lane. Harry dropped his stick, ran indoors and collapsed into his mother's apron. His father followed him in, trying to explain but Harry's mother waved him away. But for Harry, worse than the terror of the moment, was seeing his father seated in the kitchen, head in hands, weeping. Harry broke into a cold sweat as he remembered the incident and all the sensations of it came flooding back.

The gunman was sitting down on the bench opposite like an art lover who wanted to savour a particular painting.

'What's your name?'

'Harry. My name's Harry. Harry Dymond.'

'Okay, Harry, this is what we're going to do. I don't know you and I don't want to harm you. If I get what I want, nobody gets hurt.'

Harry looked around him. What could this man want? Was he going steal a painting? Surely not. You don't burst into a gallery in the middle of the day and try and steal a painting. But he felt relieved that his imminent death was at least postponed for the moment. He tried to look at the gunman without appearing to stare at him. Mid thirties maybe. Close cropped hair. Pasty face. Nondescript really. Certainly not the face of a terrorist.

'I'm Jeff, by the way, if you want to put a name to the face you're staring at.'

'Sorry, didn't mean to…'

Harry's radio crackled into life and Jeff picked it up.

'No, I'll do the talking if you don't mind. Yes, he's with me. In shock I think but he's okay. No, there's nobody else. Just the two of us. Now listen. It's about 11.30. I'm going to give you an hour and in that time you're going to bring my wife and my kids here. You're going to let me talk to them for as long I want and then, and only then, will I give myself up. If you mess me about, I'm going to blow this place up and poor old Harry goes up with me. And all these lovely paintings, too. Here's my wife's number…'

Harry listened as Jeff carefully dictated the phone number to the police. 'La Parisienne', enveloped in all her luscious blue finery continued to fix her black eyes on Harry and to smile down at him where he sat. Harry decided to venture a conversation.

'Are you 'Fathers For Justice'?'

Jeff laughed. 'No, I'm a father for justice. Just me on my own, fighting my own battle and – so far, so good – winning.'

'But, if the police comply…' Harry knew in his mind that the authorities would never place a mother and children alone with such a desperate man…'if they comply, you'll get sent down anyway, won't you?'

Jeff's face hardened and Harry wished he'd kept his mouth shut. Before Jeff could speak, Harry tried another tack.

'Tell me about your children – boys, girls?'

'One of each. Nathan's six and Zoë's four. Look, don't try the old soft soap with me. Let's just wait, shall we?'

The gallery was not a place where noise intruded to any extent. Its vast spaces with their high ceilings encouraged among visitors a reverence and quietude usually reserved for places of worship. Even parties of schoolchildren, excited to be let loose from the classroom to satisfy the module devoted to art and culture, would fall under the gallery's spell as they were shepherded around. But the silence that now wrapped itself around Harry as he sat motionless in the middle of the room was almost tangible, like being swathed from head to toe in the most delicate muslin. He could almost hear his body at rest, like a car idling at traffic lights.

But at least he felt calmer now and there was growing in him a feeling that he could not remain passive in this situation. He knew he could not control the situation he found himself in and the chances were that he was going to die. But the hopelessness of his plight, like a blank canvas, gave him choices and, if he had choices, he was still alive.

It was Jeff who broke the silence. He was walking around the room, moving from painting to painting, pausing at each work and studying it with apparent interest, like a connoisseur.

'Never seen so many pictures. How much is all this lot worth?'

'They're priceless,' said Harry, 'absolutely priceless.'

'People always say that about art and stuff but it's stupid. Everything's got a price. What about that big one behind you – the girl in blue – what's that worth?'

'La Parisienne?' asked Harry. 'One of Renoir's paintings went for £100 million a few years ago, so this one could be worth the same.'

Jeff seemed unimpressed. '£100 million and she ain't that good looking. How did this museum manage to buy all these at those kind of prices?'

'It didn't. Most of these paintings were given to the museum.'

'What, for nothing? Blimey, whoever gave these pictures must have been rolling in it. Some sort of tax dodge, was it?'

'No, they were just donated, given to the people of Wales by two sisters who loved Impressionist paintings and who bought them because they were wealthy enough to do so.'

'Impresh-what?'

'Impressionists. They were 19th century French painters. They painted in a style that was very unconventional for the time...'

This was bizarre. The knowledge he loved to impart to visitors he was now offering to a bomber who could wipe out one of the finest collection of French art outside London.

'They were called Impressionists as a kind of an insult at first but the name stuck. In the beginning they certainly weren't popular with the critics but people began to appreciate them later on. There were these two wealthy sisters, spinsters actually, and they collected these paintings when they were worth far less than they are now. They had their own private art collection and as they grew older they felt that they would like to share them with the people of Wales. So the Davies sisters gave them to the museum'

'Davies? Did you say Davies? My name's Davies. Do you think they might be related to me? That would be good, wouldn't it? Part of these paintings could belong to me. That's a laugh, that is.'

The radio buzzed. Jeff picked it up. He didn't like what he heard and his demeanour changed in a second.

'Look, you don't seem to be listening. Don't give me any bollocks about not being able to find her. You've got her and she's not keen on coming. But if you want to stop these 'priceless' paintings from being shredded, you'd better think again. You've got 30 minutes left and counting.'

Harry's stomach turned over. Jeff began pacing up and down, looking increasingly agitated. Harry's numbness returned. He thought of Molly. Would anyone have told her what was going on?

'Jeff, can I say something? The police could be lying to you, playing a game with you to see what you're

214

going to do. But it might be the truth. What if your wife isn't at home? Maybe she's out and her mobile's switched off. You've got everything under control here but maybe there's not enough time to find her. Maybe you could give them a bit more.'

'You think I'm bluffing? Think I'm scared to go through with this, do you? Look, I've got nothing to live for. The only thing I have left is my kids and if I can't see them, there's no point in going on.'

This was not the conversation Harry wanted. He felt he was contributing to Jeff's anxiety not reducing it. He didn't like the blankness he could see in Jeff's eyes. Suddenly Jeff stopped pacing and stood in front of a painting, looking at it intently.

'Did you say priceless, mate? Well this one's not even finished properly. Who the fuck painted this?'

Harry looked across to where Jeff was standing.

'That's a Van Gogh. He was a Dutch painter but he painted mostly in France.'

'Hang on, I've heard of him. Bit of a nutter, wasn't he? Cut off his own ear? How the hell can people say this is art? I wouldn't give you a tenner for it. Look, he's just scrawled great long streaks across it.'

Harry felt affronted by this comment. This was after all one of the most defining paintings of Vincent's last days but perhaps this was not the best time to open a critical dialogue in defence of one of the founding fathers of post-impressionism.

'Those streaks represent rain. He painted the cornfield just before he … and, yes, he did mutilate his ear but it was just a small piece, not his whole ear. He was going through a difficult time…'

'Like me. He lops off his lughole and I blow up this art gallery. Funny ain't it?'

'Yes, he was desperate when he painted this picture because he was passionate about painting and nobody appreciated his work. The painting sums up Vincent's despair at the time, his feelings of isolation. Yes, the brushstrokes look rough and unfinished but he's painting with his emotions. The scene is bleak with the wheeling crows and the driving rain but painting nature in all its aspects gave him strength…'

'What happened to him?' Joseph cut in. 'You said he painted this before… before what?'

Harry glanced momentarily around the gallery. The paintings seemed to be alive as he had never seen them before, their colours vibrant and pulsating as if they were breathing expectantly, waiting for an answer. He looked up at the Renoir. She was the most questioning of them all. She had finished her toilette and was dressed for the theatre in her blue dress with its enormous bustle. Her delicate hands were holding her gloves at her waist and she was perhaps glancing at herself in the mirror for one last time because some beau was already coming up the stairs to whisk her away for a night of gaiety and maybe romance in the nightspots of Montmartre. But she had a moment to spare before leaving and she, too, would like an answer to the question. She continued to look down inquisitively at the bald pate of the museum attendant seated hunched on the bench beneath her as he desperately searched his mind for an answer. 'So, Harry,' she seemed to be asking, 'what did happen to Vincent?'

Harry swallowed hard. 'On the day he painted this picture… he went back to his lodgings in the village…he was staying in a pokey room in the upstairs of a café. There was a doctor, yes, it's coming back to me now, Doctor Gachet he was called, he lived nearby

216

and he was sort of looking after Vincent because of his state of mind. Dr Gachet had rushed to the café to give Vincent a telegram. Vincent had a brother called Theo who was an art dealer. Theo was always trying to sell Vincent's paintings but without success. But this day was different because the telegram said that Theo had a buyer for five of Vincent's paintings. Well, of course, Vincent couldn't believe it at first but it was true. He thought that he would never sell anything, he thought he was worthless but he had kept on believing, kept on hoping and in the end … in the end he realised that life is always worth living.'

'So, that's how he became famous?'

'Yes, that's exactly it. Vincent's work became really popular and he sold lots more paintings. Everybody wanted a painting by Vincent and they didn't mind what they paid. He married Dr Gachet's daughter, Marguerite, and as they say lived happily ever happy. That's the whole point about this painting and that's why it's so famous because it depicts a man at the end of his rope, at a point where people would normally give up and decide …' Harry got shakily to his feet and looked up into Jeff's eyes …'decide to end it all but Vincent didn't give up on himself or what he was seeking. He kept on trying, he wouldn't give up.'

Harry sat back down exhausted. La Parisienne looked at him even more quizzically as Jeff sat down next to him and began unbuttoning his coat, an action that alarmed Harry even more.

'Look, Harry, I've got to go through with this. I mean I had to do something to see my kids. My wife has told all sorts of lies about me and I'm not allowed access on my own. So I thought I had to do something. I've tried everything.'

Jeff removed the heavy overcoat, revealing the bomb vest. Harry could see that the shirt underneath was wringing with sweat and he wondered whether the wetness could trigger the device. Didn't water act as a conduit for electrical current?

'This isn't a bomb,' said Jeff, slipping off the vest and dropping it on the floor with a dull thud. 'But this gun is real, okay, just in case you get any ideas. I thought the bomb would, you know, have more of an effect. But as far as the police know, I've still got a bomb, okay?'

'Why won't they let you see your kids? Apart from holding me hostage and threatening to blow up the museum, you seem quite a nice bloke to me.'

'It's my wife. She tells all sorts of bad stuff about me. I admit that I've had my bad moments. I had a bit of a drink problem when we were married but, there again, so did she. She cleaned up her act because they threatened to take the kids away. I took a bit longer, I know, but I've got it licked now, well, it's under control. I've got a steady job. Doesn't pay too well but I'm managing and I'm paying maintenance regular, which a lot of blokes don't. I just want us to be a family again, to get back to where we were. But she's got this fancy man that she says she's going to marry. I don't think she loves him though. She's just getting at me. If I can't have her back, I just want to see my kids.'

'What made you think about doing this in the Museum?'

Jeff looked a little sheepish and would not meet Harry's gaze. Harry wondered if he had said the right thing because his captor had calmed down considerably and he did not want him to become anxious again.

'The thing is, I didn't mean to come in here. I meant to do all this in the Law Courts. It's the lawyers who are stopping me from seeing my kids. I asked a mate of mine where the courts were and he said, you can't miss it, there's the Law Courts, City Hall and the Museum all in a row. But when I stood in front of them I couldn't remember which order they were in and, well I can't read, you see, so I had to take a guess. I knew I would only get one chance, so I ran up the steps and straight in. Before anyone could stop me I ran up the stairs and, of course, I soon realised – what with all the paintings and stuff, and there being nobody walking about with wigs on – that I'd got the wrong building. That's the story of my life, that is – always getting things wrong and making a fool of myself, unlike that Vincent bloke, never getting that break that changes things. I should just put this gun to my head and finish it.'

In spite of the ever-present danger of the situation, Harry had to smile inwardly. Trust me to get a gunman on my watch and an illiterate one at that.

'Look, Jeff,' Harry began, 'I don't think you're making a fool of yourself. You're making a stand for something you feel passionately about, just like Vincent did. You're making a stand for your kids in the same way that Vincent made a stand for his art. The important thing is what you do now. Like Vincent, you are at the end of your tether but to kill yourself is not the way out. Your kids are young now and don't understand what's happening but when they grow up, do you want them to think that their father gave up on them, didn't keep fighting for them but just blew his brains out? Surely you want them to respect you and to do that you've got to keep fighting but not in this way. You've got to give yourself up before this ends in a prolonged siege with hundreds of policemen outside and you get banged up for years. You've got to walk out with dignity; I'll stand alongside you and we'll go out together. And when they take you in I'll speak up for you. I'll tell them what you told me about how frustrated you've been and that you never intended to cause any harm. You were just a man at the end of his rope, like Vincent, and now you've made your protest for all the other fathers in your situation and you'll take what's coming to you. What do you say?'

'I don't know. I wanted this to end in a better solution but it hasn't.'

'This is better than shooting yourself and depriving your kids of their father. This is better than getting killed by a police marksman with an itchy trigger finger. You've drawn attention to your plight. Nobody's got hurt, apart from nearly giving me a heart attack, and you have told the world how you feel. Let me get on the radio and tell them we're coming out.'

Jeff said nothing but his hunched shoulders and air of defeat told Harry that it was over.

'Shall I take the gun from you?'

'No! We go out together and I'll give it up when I think it's safe.'

Harry knew this was not the best way to exit from the siege but he had no choice. He radioed the police and they said that they had to come out with hands up. If Jeff pointed the gun he risked being shot.

Harry tried to keep calm. Dealing with Jeff inside the gallery seemed easier than walking to freedom with so many guns aimed at them. He still tried to persuade Jeff to leave the gun in the gallery but there was nothing doing.

Harry exited first, moving very slowly, with Jeff so close behind him that he could feel his moist, rank breath on the back of his neck. As soon as they were in view of the police, who were crouched in the corridor and on the stairs, Jeff got agitated and Harry could sense it in his rapid breathing. The police were shouting at them both but the words were incomprehensible, something about keeping their hands in the air, which Harry was doing because he could feel his muscles stiffen into a dull ache. Some more words, just to Harry this time. What were they saying? Drop to the floor? He couldn't take it in. He could feel the blood draining from him, just as he'd felt when the gunman burst in. He knew the feeling but he had to keep standing, keep walking. *Drop to the floor, Harry, drop to the floor.* Was he saying this or was it the police? It didn't matter any more. He could feel his knees buckling under him, feel the life draining away, his head lolling and then he was gone, falling forward, gently floating down to the cool, oh so cool, marble floor.

Harry didn't hear Jeff shouting at him to get up, didn't hear the police yelling at Jeff to drop the gun, to keep his hands in the air. Harry didn't see Jeff lower his arm, not with any intent, but in a blind panic, didn't see him wheel around, didn't hear the single shot ring out and Jeff fall backwards, his chest an explosion of red. The policeman who first checked Jeff found a fluttering pulse but he was only seconds away from death. In his testimony to the Coroner, the officer said the deceased uttered only two words before expiring. The words were indistinct but he was pretty sure that Jeff's last words were, 'Sorry, Vincent.'

221

Dear Leonard,

Are you there? You'll have to forgive me if what I'm going to say makes little sense. I'm struggling to make sense of it myself. I'm in a strange place at the moment – it's like a mental no-man's-land and I'm stuck in a shell-hole, not knowing whether to go forward or back. I'm being bombarded by words and images and I know I should do something but for the moment staying put seems to be the best option.

For a while there I thought I was dead. I heard the shot and I remember falling. I thought I'd been hit and this was the end. But I remember thinking that if this was death I've had worse days. The floor felt so inviting and my body seemed to be absorbing its marbled coolness, drawing it through my veins to every part of me. It was an exhilarating feeling, Leonard. As the coolness took occupation of my body, everything else moved out – all my fears, cares and frustrations were leaching out. I was being stripped bare of all my emotions and the only sensation that was being left in me was peace, perfect peace. And if this peace was to be mine for an eternity or for just a few seconds, it was fine with me. Death could be my dominion and I would be content.

You see I'd been there before, when I was a kid. I was about seven and the country was gripped by an epidemic called Asian Flu. Everyone was dropping like flies and I caught it. My father carried my bed downstairs because we only had the one fire in the house. My mother slept in an armchair and never left my side. I got worse and the doctor was called. I remember him in a haze and my mother whispering to me that I was going to hospital to get better. Everything would be fine and she would visit me and I was to be good for the doctors and nurses. I don't remember the

222

journey but what happened after that left an indelible mark on me. I was too young to understand that I might die but that's exactly what was happening to me. I was being rushed to hospital and the safety of an oxygen tent. But all I remember in my semi-conscious state was the sensation of blissful calm. I felt no discomfort and when I awoke within the plastic cocoon that was to be my home for days I felt cheated because I wanted to continue my journey to mortality. As I say, I didn't know I was dying but when I'd recovered my mother, in a hushed breath, would tell and re-tell the story to family and visitors about how the doctor had said that he only had twenty minutes to get me into an oxygen tent or else. I wasn't supposed to be listening to all this but of course I heard it all and I wanted my mother to explain the 'or else'. What did it mean? Or else what? And then one day it hit me. Suddenly I was confronted by my own mortality. I had experienced what it felt like to nearly die and I wasn't afraid of it. The realisation that you can die does not occupy the thoughts of most seven year olds as they climb trees and kick footballs around. But I was a strange little boy, Leonard, and I felt somehow strengthened by my experience. Maybe it was just morbid curiosity but when I thought that I had been killed in the museum I was happy to embrace it.

But of course my luck ran out and I regained consciousness in the back of the ambulance. Molly was sitting beside me but her head was in her hands and she didn't see me open my eyes. I glanced at her and as she turned to look at me I shut my eyes again and tried to go back. I was saying it was okay. I didn't mind dying. What was there to worry about? I felt Molly's hand grip mine tightly. She was murmuring something that I couldn't quite make out and, anyway, the spell was broken by now and I knew that I wasn't going to depart the land of the living. I opened my eyes and we looked at each other. I searched for words but none came. Molly just wept and said: 'Harry, I thought I'd lost you, you ninny.'

So I hadn't ventured into the undiscovered country. I had just fainted and banged my head on the floor, leaving me with mild concussion. But I'm still adrift, Leonard, still searching for that haven. Maybe death is not the solution. Maybe I'll just have to wait my turn and, instead of a short, sharp death, I will have the slow inexorable death of dementia, sitting in my incontinence pants in one of those dreadful wing chairs being spoon-fed rice pudding by a care assistant who wishes she'd worked harder in school.

So you see, Leonard, even the experience of surviving a hostage situation has not left me feeling much happier. What worries me now is my return to normality. Molly is keeping me in purdah because she knows that's what I want. But I'm going to have to face the world at some time and she tells me that there's an army of media people wanting a slice of me. I don't want to be a nine-day wonder, Leonard, satisfying the media's desire to give the public a feel-good story with a long enough shelf life until the next one appears. I want to return to the mediocre obscurity that I have cultivated all these years. You understand, don't you? You've taken time out from your life in order to find some kind of inner peace, haven't you? Well, I want nothing more than to go back to my mundane world but maybe to appreciate more the life I had and to try harder to be tolerant of the things I can't change. Does that make sense, Leonard?

CHAPTER 25

Harry spent the next few days at home with the curtains drawn. He couldn't cope with all the media interest surrounding the incident at the museum. For a few days Harry Dymond was a national celebrity but he refused all demands for a television interview. The museum was quick to extol the coolness and bravery of its member of staff. He received a personal message from the director who told him he could take as much paid leave as he wanted in order to recover from his ordeal. A couple of his friends went on camera to say what a good bloke he was and the school where Harry had worked wanted him to be its guest of honour at the next speech day. Eventually, for the sake of getting the media off his back, Molly persuaded him to be interviewed by the South Wales Echo, which published an article complete with photo entitled 'The Modest Hero'.

Molly took some time off work, but she left Harry to himself most of time. She could see that he wanted to cocoon himself for the present and knew that this was his way of coping. Her job was to protect him from all the telephone calls and keep visitors at bay. She did not speak to Harry about the incident; she would wait until he was ready. They would sit together in silence of an evening just watching the television but she could see that Harry was staring beyond the screen into a world in which he was momentarily lost.

About a week later, as Molly was making a cup of tea to take up to Harry in bed, he came into the kitchen and asked if she'd like to go for a drive down to the Bay for a coffee and maybe a stroll along the Barrage. Molly gazed intently at his face, not knowing what signs she was seeking to find there. He still looked very haggard, like a POW just released from captivity.

'I'm okay now,' he said with a slight smile. 'I think I'll go back to work next week. I'll give them a ring later.'

~

Harry and Molly had walked about halfway across the Barrage and were now huddled under an awning of white sailcloth on a bench overlooking the freshwater lake and opposite the skyline of modern buildings that were the centrepieces of the new Cardiff Bay. A freshening breeze was whipping up the slate-coloured water into zesty waves that lapped against the edge of the Barrage. From where Harry and Molly sat, the only visible remnant of Cardiff's history as the world's greatest coal-exporting port was the Pierhead building, its red brickwork glowing in a shaft of welcome January sunshine on an otherwise chilly afternoon. Behind the Pierhead, and dwarfing it, stood the Millennium Centre, its roof a burnished gold in the sunlight, while to the side loomed the Senedd, the home of Wales's experiment in political autonomy. A visitor might have suggested that the white Norwegian church surely deserved a mention for its 19th century origins but Harry would have pointed out that, while it was indeed built in the era of King Coal, it used to occupy a site near the dock entrance and the decision to relocate the church where Roald Dahl once worshipped reflected aesthetic rather than historical considerations.

They had passed only a few words all afternoon but Molly was untroubled by Harry's silence. In light of recent events, it was a relief to be out of doors with him. There was time enough for talking later. Molly's thoughts drifted back to the past and she wasn't really aware that she was articulating her memories.

226

'Harry, do you remember Cardiff when we were first at university? Tiger Bay was a no-go area then. We were told not to venture down the Docks for fear of being robbed or raped or worse. I'd seen that film with Hayley Mills – you remember, she witnesses this murder and is trying to protect this seaman – what was his name? – oh yes, Horst Bucholtz. I loved that film and I wanted to see what Butetown was really like but no one would go with me. People said that policemen in the docks always went around in threes and there were crooks and prostitutes around every corner. But I was determined to go and I managed to persuade two other girls to come with me.

'It was a pretty grim area, I must admit. It was neglected and run down but that's because it had fallen on hard times. Anyway, we found a pub and plucked up courage to go in. There was live music playing and everyone looked at us as we entered. We must have looked pretty incongruous because I think we all had uni scarves on. But everyone was really friendly and we had a great time. The people in the pub were rough and ready and I had trouble understanding what some of them were saying because their accents were strange to me, but I remember thinking that here was a community that had been the lifeblood of Cardiff and now they were on the ropes because the docks had had its day. But it was a real community, proud and above all alive, with such a diverse culture. Before all this talk of racial equality, here was a model of how different races could live together in some sort of harmony. And yet, the powers-that-be didn't seem to care about what happened to Butetown.

'And now Tiger Bay is Cardiff Bay but have the people of Butetown benefited from all these changes? Is it their patch any more? Excuse the cliché but do they have *ownership* of all this? Look at it now. Iconic buildings, bijou apartments and trendy bars and restaurants. An area that was once filled with a rough but vibrant community has been turned into a middle-class lifestyle theme park. Haven't we lost something here? What do *you* think, Harry?'

'Yes, it's great, isn't it? What an improvement.'

~

It was the Saturday before Harry was due back at the museum and he was busying himself in the garage. There was nothing to be busy about because the garage was still in pristine order. Surgeons would have happily performed open-heart surgery in there. But there was always the floor to sweep and while he went through the motions his thoughts returned to recent events.

What a crazed notion for Jeff to embark upon! That storming the museum would allow him access to his kids. Emotion had driven all reason out of his mind and the only consequence had been his futile death. To what lengths are people driven when they are pushed to the limits? Harry wondered if he could have done more for Jeff or perhaps even less? Should he have just kept his mouth shut instead of pouring all that nonsense about Vincent's alternative life? Should he have just waited until trained negotiators came on the scene? Would Jeff be alive if he had just kept silent? Modest hero, my arse! Bungling idiot, more like.

Harry decided to raise the garage door to let the dust out and was surprised to see a removal van on next door's drive. Two men were struggling to get a large wardrobe into the house. Normally Harry would have walked over to introduce himself to the new neighbour but he didn't feel quite ready yet for social pleasantries.

He was about to retreat back into the garage when a man of roughly his own age emerged from the house and immediately caught Harry's eye. He smiled at Harry and began to walk over. There was no escape so Harry quickly tried to compose himself.

'Hello, said Harry, offering his hand. 'Nice to meet you. The name's Harry, Harry Dymond.'

'Nice to meet you, too. Joe… Joe Barker.'

Harry felt the breath leave his body and an all too familiar feeling made his legs give way.

'You okay, mate? You look like you need to sit down. Come inside a minute. I'll make you a cuppa. You'll have to excuse all the mess.'

Harry allowed himself to be taken by the arm as Joe led him into the house. He sat quietly in the kitchen while Joe made a pot of tea. He realised that this was the first time he had entered Mr Barker's house, his former neighbour having been the most private of men. The kitchen looked unchanged from the fifties with its black and white chequered floor tiles and its walls covered in faded wallpaper covered with pineapples jostling for space with ripe bananas and the occasional utensil. On an old three-ringed cooker Joe was trying to coax a kettle to come to the boil. It will all have to be gutted, thought Harry, as he collected his thoughts once more. The kettle suddenly gave out a shrill whistle that made Harry jump.

'There you go,' said Joe, placing a cup of tea in Harry's hands. 'Do you have turns like these often? You had me going there for a minute.'

Harry took a sip of his tea and felt the hot liquid flow through him. He tried to speak but the words were slow to come.

'It's just … I mean, I thought you were … dead.'

Harry took a gulp of his tea and, with more coherence, told Joe all about the photos that Molly had rescued and the search to unravel the mystery of the MG Midget. Joe was taken aback by the meticulous lengths to which Harry had gone.

'I just can't believe I got this all wrong,' said Harry. 'I was convinced that Mr Barker's son had been killed in a car crash, not that I wanted you to die, you understand. I was so shocked to see you just now. But what I don't understand is the car itself. It was in a crash, wasn't it?

Joe remained silent for what seemed like an age and swallowed hard before replying.

'You're right about the crash and I was in the car at the time but I survived. The driver didn't.'

'You weren't driving the car? But who was?'

Joe's eyes were quickly filling up. 'It was my mother. It was she who was driving the car when it crashed. I was taking her for a spin and she kept asking if she could have a go. She'd driven in the war, she said. I knew that sometimes she took my father's car to the shops, so I thought it would be all right. But she lost control and crashed into a verge. The car didn't have seat belts and she got thrown from the car. She didn't stand a chance. My father never forgave me and refused to speak to me or have me in the house after that. So I ended up moving away and eventually emigrated to Canada. My father was a very proud man and I knew that he was never going to back down. I should have come home sooner, I know, but I guess I'm more like him than I like to think. I didn't know that he had succumbed to dementia and I suppose I'm going to have to live with this guilt for the rest of my life.'

Harry knew that he had to say something or an agonising pause would ensue.

'Do you want the photos?'

'What?'

'The photos of your family that my wife dug out of the skip. She was the one who started me on this so-called mystery. She didn't want your family's memories ending up on a rubbish heap. It might be painful to look at them again but they are your photos and you should have them. Shall I bring them round when you're settled in?'

'Thank you,' smiled Joe. 'I'd like that very much.'

Harry got up to leave but stopped. He had one question of Joe that he knew he shouldn't ask but his curiosity was pressing him.

'I know this is none of my business but can I ask … what happened to the girl in the photo, you know, she's posing on the car's bonnet?'

Joe gave Harry a blank stare as if the answer could be found in the furrows of his neighbour's brow. And then something clicked into place. 'Oh, you mean Clare, my girlfriend. You've got that photo? We were quite stuck on each other at the time. Well, I was pretty smitten with her. We'd met at university and I suppose in time we would have married. That photo was taken a few days before the accident. Clare had gone to visit her parents and I was thankful that she was spared the whole tragic episode. We talked on the phone and I fully expected her to come back, at least for the funeral, but she didn't and I never saw her again. I think she just couldn't cope with it and, of course, I could forgive her for that, even though it made me feel all the more guilty. It was as if my mother's death was now attached to me forever like a stigma and she was never going to handle it. That's when I decided to go to Canada and make a new start of everything. It's funny but I'd forgotten all about Clare. She was a lovely girl and I messed up everything between us. A mutual friend told me years later that she married a vet and moved to the Peak District. I hope she's had a happy life.'

Dear Leonard,

What an idiot you must think I am. I spend all these weeks obsessing about this Joe, like some amateur sleuth in a detective story, stepping in to solve the mystery that is beyond the faculties of a host of flat-footed Mr Plods. When Molly rescued those photos from the skip, it was an act of pure kindness in memory of a neighbour, a simple emotional response. But I have to view them in a completely different light, as a mystery that only my intellect can unravel. I snatch at a theory to solve the puzzle and then fit the evidence to make it true, except of course that I'm totally wrong and Joe turns up, large as life, and no doubt wondering whether moving next door to a pompous prat like me was such a good idea.

Why do I do this all the time? Why am I always so blinkered and single-minded in everything I do? I'm like the captain of a doomed liner, shouting full steam ahead from the bridge, ignoring the warnings of my officers about the rather large white icy thing lying straight ahead. Is this why I have so few friends? I know that I can come across as quite superior and nobody likes a know-all, do they? And it's true that I rarely take anyone's advice but I like dispensing my own opinions. Oh God, I've just realised that I wouldn't like me if I met me for the first time.

I'm beginning to think that Molly has been a saint to put up with me all these years. She said once that I'm like an island connected by a causeway to the mainland that is our relationship. Most of the time she can cross the causeway and enjoy my company but when the tide within me is at the full, its breakers crashing against the shoreline, she cannot make the crossing. She can only stand listlessly on the shore watching me in my own world until the tide ebbs and she can revisit me. I've

233

taken her too much for granted over the years and I must try to make amends. I don't know how but I must try.'

Harry was visiting Paul for the first time since the museum incident. Paul had asked him to come over for the afternoon. Harry agreed with some reluctance because he was still not ready to resume what little social life he had. He did not feel comfortable talking about the incident that inevitably was the main source of conversation amongst his few acquaintances. When he arrived at the house, Paul was standing next to the MG Midget, which was now parked on the drive. They shook hands.

'I suppose I should ask you for your autograph. I saw it all on BBC Wales. You're a hero, Harry.'

'I'm no hero. It all went wrong. The guy shouldn't have been killed. The gun was just a replica. He meant no harm.'

'But you didn't know that and neither did the police. They had to do what they did. Once you dived to the ground, they had to take him out. By all accounts, he was acting like a lunatic and he could have killed someone...'

'...if the gun was real, but it wasn't. And I didn't dive to the ground; I fainted. I fainted away like a granny with the vapours. That's not heroic.'

Paul took Harry by the shoulders and stared into his eyes.

'Look, Harry, that's rubbish. This guy has a bomb strapped to him and is carrying a gun. That's what you believe to be true. You kept him calm. You kept him from blowing you and the whole museum to kingdom come. That's all you need to know and that's what the public think. You're a brave man, Harry, whatever you may think of yourself. Anyway, let's enjoy the day. I'm really glad you could come. I just thought if I was taking her out for a spin, you might like to come along. In the summer, I normally have the top down but it's a bit nippy for that today. Jump in.'

In spite of their unfortunate first meeting, Harry and Paul were becoming good friends. Harry found the younger man very easy to get on with. He was a successful businessman but there was nothing brash about him. Harry had already had a couple of lessons with Ralph and that had started well. He had slipped back into a teaching role with surprising ease and he was enjoying helping a boy whose problem was not a poor grasp of the subject but having the confidence to express himself.

Paul switched on the engine and it purred into life. 'I had it mot'd yesterday and it sailed through. I thought we'd take it along the A48 and then down the lanes to Llantwit Major. Okay with you?'

Harry didn't mind where he went. It was a clear but cold day and a drive in the country might clear some of the anxious cobwebs that still clouded his mind. Wilkins couldn't believe how Harry had extracted the name Ian Russell from Alex's guest book entry.

'You ought to work for MI5, Harry,' he had said. 'Working out that name from Alex's spelling mistakes was just awesome. But I don't get this 'Jack Hughes' thing. How did you work out that she was saying, what was it, *J'accuse*?'

'Alex had dropped hints about Emile Zola. Zola wrote a famous article called *J'accuse* or *I accuse* in English, in defence of an army officer who had been wrongly convicted of treason. It caused a sensation at the time and eventually helped to get the verdict overturned. Alex had cleverly planted Zola in my mind and so I made the link when I saw the name Jack Hughes.'

'So, this Zola chap. Is he anything to do with Gianfranco Zola, you know, the footballer?'

'I think they could be cousins,' said Harry, allowing himself a smile. 'Emile Zola was a bit of a midfield dynamo but an injury put him out of the game and so he turned to writing for a living.'

Wilkins thought that Alex had concocted the entry as a sort of insurance policy, trying to make sure that the authorities had a name if anything ever happened to her. It was a long shot, Wilkins said, but she was probably getting desperate and this guy Ian Russell wasn't keen to let her go. The name itself did not produce a ready suspect. It was not an uncommon name and the police computer had thrown up dozens of possibilities. Some had been easily eliminated for either being dead or in jail. The background of other Ian Russells didn't quite fit the picture. Some were petty criminals whose activities were unlikely to extend to stealing antiquarian books and, of course, this guy might not have a criminal record or he could be using an alias.

However, Wilkins had found one Ian Russell who had form and who just might be the man. He had a criminal record for handling stolen goods, usually of the upmarket type, rich pickings from houses in the stockbroker belt and the apartments of the wealthy in central London. Wilkins thought that he would have the contacts to start something on his own and, tellingly, he had one conviction for arson, setting fire to the flat of a former accomplice who had failed to repay a debt. Russell's stamping ground was also interesting because he lived in Portchester in a house that stood right on the edge of Portsmouth harbour and it even had his own mooring for a boat. It was Wilkins who had spotted another clue in Alex's entry in the guest book. Alex had underlined the letters p-o-r-t in the place name, St Quay

Portrieux. A definite pointer to Portchester, he said. If Alex had been using the ferries from St Malo, Cherbourg and Caen to bring across the goods, Russell could actually look from the large bay window of his house and see the ferries docking in the harbour. A quick exchange with Alex and she could be up the M27 on her way to Witney while he stashed the goods in Portchester ready for moving them to wherever they were destined. 'I can feel it my water,' said Wilkins. 'It's got to be him.' Harry thought that only TV policemen had hunches but in this case the hunch was actually fruitless because when they raided Russell's house it was empty with everything cleared out.

'Am I boring you, Harry?' said Paul, as the car came to a halt just outside Cowbridge on the A48.

'Sorry?' Harry came back with a jolt

'I've been talking to myself for the last ten minutes. You were so deep in thought. Anyway, your turn now. Out you get.'

Harry protested. He did not want to drive Paul's car, Paul's father's precious vehicle and at one time Joe's wheels. But Paul would have none of it and he bundled Harry into the driver's seat.

'Just take it easy to start with and then we'll slip off the main road and head for Llantwit. C'mon, you'll enjoy it. She's a beauty to drive.'

Harry switched on the ignition and carefully eased the car into motion. It picked up speed very quickly and he had to watch the speedometer at first. But it wasn't long before he felt his shoulder muscles relax and he leaned back in his seat.

'Where shall I go?' asked Harry, as he grew more confident with the car's handling.

'Let the car decide. Just turn off the main road when it feels right and let the car have its head. Harry kept the car on the A48 for the next few miles and then a road sign intrigued him. He turned left and headed down a series of winding lanes. The car gripped the road like it was stuck to it and soon Harry was enjoying the twisting lanes as they undulated through the Vale of Glamorgan. But he still had to concentrate hard, so much so that it was Paul and not Harry who noticed the black car behind them.

'What's that silly bugger trying to do? There's no way he can pass us here.'

Harry gave a nervous glance in his rear-view mirror. The black car was right on his bumper. Then there was a nudge that made Harry's hands shudder on the steering wheel, causing the Midget to swerve wildly from side to side. They came to a wider section of the road and Paul shouted, 'Let him pass, Harry! Let the maniac pass!' But the black car only pulled alongside and Harry knew that it was not a boy racer looking for some sport at their expense. This car had a more deadly objective. Harry pushed hard down on the accelerator and the Midget sped off. Paul was screaming at him to slow down but Harry knew that somehow he had to outrun the black car. He took the next bend with the tyres screeching in protest. If a car had been coming in the opposite direction they would have been done for. The black car was picking up speed again and Harry could see it looming ever larger in his mirror. Ahead he could see a sign indicating a right turn. He waited until he was level and then turned the steering wheel frantically at the last moment sending the car spinning down the lane. He glanced at his mirror and was mortified to see the black car still behind. It had struggled to make the turn but was now gathering speed. Paul was still screaming at Harry to stop but it was futile. The road was widening out again and Harry

239

knew that the black car would try to force them off the road. He accelerated and the other car responded, nudging the bumper and then creeping alongside. Harry looked ahead. At the end of the straight road Harry could just see the chevrons that indicated a sharp left bend. As the black car started to edge along the side of the Midget, Harry accelerated again and the black car roared alongside. Just as Harry approached the bend, he slammed on the brakes in a haze of tyre smoke and saw the black car speed pass him, veering wildly from side to side as the driver, trying to take the bend too quickly, lost control and ploughed straight into the bank, smashing into a wooden fence, the back end spinning round until the car finally came to a halt, its front end facing them.

Paul and Harry raced from the Midget. The front of the BMW had taken most of the impact, the windscreen had shattered and the air bag had inflated. It was difficult to see the driver at first. Harry thought that the air bag had probably saved him from the worst of the impact and it had. He was still in his seat looking for all the world as if he had just nodded off but then they noticed that the broken fence had left its mark, for a shattered piece of wood was embedded in his chest. Harry looked to the man's face for a sign of the horror of the wound that had just killed him outright but across the dead man's features was merely a look of mild surprise as if someone had just told him a very interesting fact about Namibia.

~

Harry and Paul were sitting in the kitchen of a large house, set back from the road, a couple of hundred yards from the crash. An attending paramedic had given them a routine once-over. They were both in shock but Harry more so. However, he refused to be taken to

240

hospital. He just wanted to get home to Molly but the police had told them to hang on in case there were further questions. So they were relieved when the house's owner, Mrs Wetherby, offered them a cup of tea while they waited. She had been exercising her horse in the adjacent paddock and had rushed to the scene when she heard the crash. As Harry sipped his sweet tea, he watched her as she bustled about the scrubbed pine kitchen, wittering away about how the horse had reared at the noise of screeching tyres and buckled metal, very nearly throwing her. She was at least ten years older than Harry and, even in her own kitchen, looked incongruous in riding britches and boots.

'More tea, chaps? There's plenty in the pot.' Then looking directly at Harry: 'You look like you could do with something stronger. You're not going to faint away on me, are you? What does one do? Ah yes, head between the knees or is that for nose bleeds? Never can remember.'

'I'm fine, thank you,' said Harry, but I'd love another cup.'

Just then, Harry's mobile rang and he felt comforted to hear a familiar voice.

'It's Russell all right,' Wilkins said after enquiring if Harry was all right. 'South Wales Police have identified him and the car was registered in his name. You were lucky, Harry, but it begs the question why Ian Russell was going after you when you had nothing on him and he's eliminated the only person who had. Have you been holding something back?'

Harry told Wilkins about the photos Russell had taken in Bristol and the note he had received.

241

'You're a bloody fool, Harry. You could have got killed and that other guy with you in the car. What were you thinking of?'

Harry had no explanation. He was sorry about holding back. At first he'd been afraid of being implicated and after Alex's death he realised that he might still be a target for Russell but it had all got very confused in his mind.

'Anyway, it's all over bar the shouting now,' said Wilkins. 'Case closed.' He paused for a moment before saying: 'Harry, I know we were at opposite ends when this whole sorry business started but for a while I didn't know where you stood. For all I knew you were the criminal mastermind behind it, masquerading as a complete … well, an innocent abroad might describe it better. But in the end you've come through and, well, you've earned your stripes, Harry. You're a good bloke and I'll miss our little chats. All the best and good luck.'

Just then a young police constable stuck his head around the kitchen door and told Harry and Paul they were free to go. The police would be in touch if they needed anything more. They rose from their chairs and thanked Mrs Wetherby for her hospitality. They were welcome to stay longer if they wished, she said. She didn't get many visitors these days. Harry sighed as he saw the prospect of a long life story emerging but Mrs Wetherby suddenly paused.

'Now there's a peculiar thing,' she continued. 'How could I forget that? Do you know that nearly forty years ago there was a car crash on that very same bend but there was only one car involved. A woman got thrown from the car and died at the scene. Can't remember if it was the driver or passenger. I'm trying to remember what kind of car it was. My husband would have remembered, bless him. He loved cars. It was one of those little sporty cars, I think. What do you think of that? You two were lucky today, even if the other chap wasn't, poor thing.'

Dear Leonard,

When I first spoke to you I didn't know how to start and now I don't know how to conclude. I could talk in clichés about everything being a journey and I've reached the end, having come safely to harbour. But that's a bit demeaning to someone as poetic as you.

Am I better than when I began this conversation? I think not. I still see life as a bit of a wasteland but perhaps I'm better equipped to tramp through it. Oops, there's that journey thing again.

Molly and I took a drive today. When she was doing her teacher training in the early 70s she opted for a school in the Rhondda Valley, which meant more travelling for her but she said that if we were going to spend the rest of our lives in south Wales she wanted to see as much of it as possible. The Rhondda is a former coal mining area, probably the most important mining area in Britain in its heyday. When she taught there, the coal industry was in rapid decline and it bore the scars of its glory days. She took me up there once and I was shocked, I can tell you. The place was so grim and bleak, well to me it was, coming from the countryside. Although the funny thing was there were sheep wandering around the streets of Tonypandy where she was teaching. She said it was normal and you got used to them. But, the sheep apart, what struck me was the surroundings. It seemed so rough, so hopeless and inhuman. It was February and very chilly. All the people we passed as we walked up to the town from the train station seemed downtrodden and cowed. I'm probably exaggerating here a bit because of the contrast between where I grew up and coming to the Rhondda for the first time but that's how I felt and shocked isn't too harsh a word.

But today we went to the Rhondda again for the first time since Molly's teaching practice. And I was shocked again by the changes that had taken place in forty years. All the evidence of mining had gone, except for one pithead, which was a heritage park. The narrow streets were still there, with row upon row of tiny houses clinging for dear life to the sides of the valley but instead of looking grim they were now quaint, like something from a folk museum. But what struck me most was the green. The whole valley had greened up as if someone had taken a huge paintbrush and splashed a great swathe of green right through the valley. It was unrecognisable. Nature decided to give this place a second chance and when the coal mines moved out it moved back in.

We drove through the valley, right up to where you think you can go no further, until the road takes a sharp bend and takes you over a mountain called the Rhigos, winding up and up until you leave the Rhondda behind and come to the edge of the Brecon Beacons. When we reached the peak, we stopped the car in a lay-by and got out. You could see the Brecon Beacons in all their glory stretching ahead of us for miles and miles.

I could see that Molly wanted to talk and I wasn't as resistant as I usually am. She spoke about the last few months and how she had felt really tested. By this she meant me; she didn't come straight out but I knew she meant me. She said that there had been moments when she wasn't sure if she could continue living with me. I was retreating, she said, into a place that offered her no comfort and no respite, and she was afraid to follow me. She also said that there were times when she'd lost the will to lure me back. It wasn't going to be worth the effort.

And then there was the man in the museum and the police ringing to tell her of the danger I was in. It was then that she decided that she would fight for me, not that she could do anything to help me. Nobody could. She rushed down to the museum and tried to get near but the police were keeping people away. She sat in the park opposite, right under the statue of Lloyd George shaking his fist and she said that she saw that image and clenched her own fist, saying *if you kill Harry I'll kill you* over and over to herself. *If you kill Harry I'll kill you.* And then she heard the shot and a great groan went up from the people around the museum. It was then she said that if I still lived she'd walk into that dark cave with me and live with me whatever it took.

I have to tell you, Leonard, that I wept like a baby. Something came from the very depths of my being and poured out of me in one long, agonising moan. I shook and shivered with the ache and release of it. I felt that I had let go of something that had wound itself around my soul with a hundred tentacles and it was now being expelled. Molly hugged me and said, 'Come to me, you old ninny. That's it. Let it go, let it go.'

Am I changed? Well, not completely. That would be unrealistic. What flowed from me that day was an accumulation of things that had built up within me over a very long time, things that we choose to suppress because either we can't face them or we can't deal with them, or both. A sort of catharsis, I suppose. I try harder not to be me, if that makes sense. Molly helps me. She gives me a look if we're in company and I'm just about to launch into something pompous and pedantic. And I try harder to empathise with other people but that's not easy. And some days I'm the Harry of old and I can't stop myself.

The situation in the museum is better. Meera says I've got street cred after the incident and my workmates respect me more. Paul helps me, too. I still teach his son history and I think he'll get at least a pass in history but I'm hoping for better. Paul sold the Midget, by the way, because he said he thought it was spooked and he hoped his father wouldn't mind.

So I feel that I have been dragged from the wreckage that was my life. I have moved on and that's got a lot to do with you. You've been a good listener, Leonard, and an even greater support. I don't know what you've thought of my ramblings over the past few months but it's got me through, I can tell you. So I'm going to sign off this one-sided correspondence and just say… thanks.

Is there a message in all this? I don't think so, Leonard, at least not one that is universal. Have I learned anything? I've learned acceptance. What you can't change, you have to live with. But you taught me that years ago.

I wish I could write like you, Leonard. I wish I could see the world as you see it. You've given me so much but, above all, you've given me a mantra to comfort all the lost souls like me. You know what I mean, don't you Leonard? It's been my lodestar for a long time and it's the only fundamental truth that I believe in.

Shall we say it together, Leonard? I'd like that.

There's a crack, a crack in everything, that's how the light gets in.

Lightning Source UK Ltd.
Milton Keynes UK
UKOW03f2118300414

230900UK00004B/267/P